D0512415

Please return / renew by date shown.
You can renew it at:
norlink.norfolk.gov.uk
or by telephone: 0344 800 8006
Please have your library card & PIN ready

NORFOLK LIBRARY
AND INFORMATION SERVICE

A Dark Touch Novel
BETRAYAL

Amy Meredith

RED FOX

DARK TOUCH: BETRAYAL
A RED FOX BOOK 978 1 849 41148 6

First published in Great Britain by Red Fox,
an imprint of Random House Children's Books
A Random House Group Company

This edition published 2011

1 3 5 7 9 10 8 6 4 2
Series created and developed by Amber Caravéo

The Random House Group Limited makes every effort to ensure that the papers
used in its books are made from trees that have been legally sourced from
well-managed and credibly certified forests. Our paper procurement policy can
be found at: www.randomhouse.co.uk/environment.

Mixed Sources
Product group from well-managed
forests and other controlled sources
www.fsc.org Cert no. TT-COC-2139
© 1996 Forest Stewardship Council

Set in 12/16pt Minion

Red Fox Books are published by Random House Children's Books,
61–63 Uxbridge Road, London W5 5SA

www.**kids**at**random**house.co.uk
www.**totally**random**books**.co.uk
www.**random**house.co.uk

Addresses for companies within The Random House Group Limited
can be found at: www.randomhouse.co.uk/offices.htm
THE RANDOM HOUSE GROUP Limited Reg. No. 954009

A CIP catalogue record for this book is available from the British Library.

Printed and bound in Great Britain by
CPI Bookmarque, Croydon, CR0 4TD

For Team Dark Touch, especially
Ruth Knowles, Jess Clarke
and Natalie Doherty.

Prologue

Killing was harder than the boy thought it would be. The knife was sharp, but his first attempt to slit the rabbit's throat only made a scratch under the soft brown fur. He'd have to do better next time.

With one hand, the boy tightened his hold on the rabbit. With the other, he tightened his hold on the knife. The animal fought harder, its powerful back legs kicking out as it struggled in the boy's grip, struggled for freedom, for life.

He didn't try to slice this time. Instead, he jabbed, and a hot, red fountain of arterial blood arched into the air. The boy turned the rabbit so that the blood splashed down into the shallow stone bowl he'd placed on the floor of the old playhouse. He tried to ignore the hard, fast thundering of the rabbit's heart – *thumpthumpthumpthump* – against his body. He tried to ignore the way those hard, fast beats slowed. Then stopped.

When the blood stopped flowing, the boy shoved the animal into the canvas bag he'd brought. Later he would place it where he needed it. But for now, he didn't want it in his sight. He knelt down in front of the bowl, dropped the knife, and used an old scrap of crayon-covered paper to scrub the wet blood off his hands. Then he reached into his backpack and pulled out the thick candles – one white, one black, one red. He lit them, then stared at them for a long moment, as if he'd forgotten what they were for or even why he was in the old playhouse at all.

He shook his head and picked the knife up again. He wiped it on the floor, then, before he had time to think about it, drew it across his thumb. He let his blood mix with the blood of the sacrifice. The red candle flared in the dark shack, casting strange shadows over the stick-figure drawings he'd hung up as a small child. He pulled a few strands of hair from his head and dropped them into the stone bowl, then used his teeth to bite off a few pieces of fingernail. He added them. The black candle flared.

The boy returned to his backpack and took out a thick book, the leather of its binding cracked with age. He turned to the page he'd marked and began to read, the strange words difficult for his mouth and tongue to form. The white candle flared.

All the candle flames were impossibly high now, as high as the kneeling boy's head, nearly reaching the ceiling of the small wooden playhouse. When he spoke the last word on the page, all the flames went out at once, the wicks emitting thin trails of dark smoke.

The boy's body shuddered. Spasms ripped through him again and again, and a howl worked its way out of his throat.

Then he went still. And silent.

He slid the ancient book back into his backpack.

It was done.

Chapter One

'Oh my God!' Jess Meredith cried from the end of the Deepdene High hallway. 'Omigod, omigod, omigod,' she continued as she raced towards Eve Evergold. 'Oh. My. God,' Jess said as she came to a stop in front of Eve's locker.

'I don't have to ask if those are good OMGs or bad ones. You should see the expression on your face – it's like you've been eating sunbeams,' Eve told her best friend. She smiled. How could she not smile when happiness was zinging out of Jess, turning her cheeks pink and making her blue eyes sparkle?

'Oh my God!' Jess squealed in reply.

'OK, I need more, even though we're telefriendic.' Telefriendic was the word she and Jess had come up with to describe the way one best friend can guess what another best friend is thinking. Eve and Jess had huge telefriendic abilities, but today Eve couldn't figure out anything other than that Jess had some-thing really good – really, really, really good – to tell her. 'I need more words. No, not just *more*.' Who knew how many times Jess could OMG? '*Different* words, please.'

Jess gave a twirl right there in the hall, like she'd suddenly become part of the cast of *Glee*. 'Evie, I'm going to the Senior Prom!' She twirled again, arms out, narrowly missing three people heading for the cafeteria. 'Seth just asked me. I was starting think maybe . . . But, no, he asked. I'm, I'm – we have to come up with a new word for how I'm feeling right now! Wowtastic, maybe. I don't know. I'm going to the Senior Prom!'

'That's so awesome!' Eve gave Jess a hug, trying to pretend that the news hadn't given her a pang – well, at least a tiny panglet – of envy and sadness. She and Jess had been talking about the Senior Prom ever since they first knew what a prom was, spinning out fantasies of what they'd wear, how they'd do their hair, where they'd go for dinner. And in all those fantasies, they were always together, sharing a limo with their dates, the four of them going down to the beach after the prom and making a bonfire. It had never occurred to her that one of them would go without the other. 'So when do we head to Manhattan to begin the dress search?' she asked, getting another panglet.

'Can we leave now?' Jess grinned. 'No, can't risk it,' she answered her own question. 'What if I got suspended for skipping school and was banned from the prom? That would be the ultimate ironic tragedy.'

'We can still strategize over lunch with Jenna and Shanna and everybody,' Eve said. This was huge for Jess, seriously huge, and Eve wasn't going to spoil it because she was having pangs – or panglets. She shut her locker, and she and Jess started for the cafeteria. 'So should we go geographical, just work our way from Bloomingdales down to SoHo?' When there was extremely serious shopping to be done, it had to be done in Manhattan. It was absolutely worth a couple of hours on the train to reach shopping nirvana.

'Or should we go to our faves first, no matter where they are?' Eve continued. 'You don't want to miss out on The Dress because someone scoops it up before you see it.'

'It's going to take more than one day,' Jess replied. 'Do you think our parents would let us stay in a hotel for a glamorous weekend of shopping?'

It wasn't as if Deepdene, their Hamptons beachside

town, didn't have a very nice selection of boutiques on Main Street. The little town had a small population – only 2,700 – but a large percentage of that 2,700 were millionaires, celebs of various types – including celebs who hadn't done anything to be celebs – and all those people liked to shop. They kept the stores on Main thriving – with a little help from Eve and Jess, who were somewhat fond of shopping themselves, even when there wasn't a prom coming up.

'Extremely dubious,' Eve said. 'But we can just make multiple trips if we have to. The prom's only two weeks away, though. We're going to have to shop harder than we ever have before.'

'I know!' Jess exclaimed. 'I can't believe Seth only asked me two weeks beforehand. I really started to think maybe he wouldn't.'

'And I told you he was just being a boy,' Eve reminded her. 'Boys are so clueless about what it takes for a girl to become prom-ready. You're lucky he didn't wait another week to ask!' she added as they entered the cafeteria and joined the food queue.

'He asked? Finally?' their friend Rose exclaimed, turning to face them. The when of Seth's prom invitation – no one doubted it would happen at some point – had been a topic of conversation at their usual table for weeks. Jess was the only one of their group of friends who was going out with a senior, and they'd all wanted to know every detail.

'At last!' Jess answered.

'Hey, Jenna,' Rose called. 'Who had today in the Seth pool?'

Jenna leaned round the two people between her and her friends, then checked her iPhone. 'What time? Megan had before school. Shanna had after homeroom.'

'That means Shanna wins,' Jess announced.

Eve and the rest of Jess's close friends had each put in twenty bucks and taken a guess at when 'The Asking' would occur. Rose gave an exaggerated pout. 'I was going to buy every eye pencil Urban Decay makes.'

'Awww. And you only have eighty million eye pencils now. How are you going to survive?' Jenna teased as they headed for their usual table.

'Oh! You should make your hair and mani-pedi appointments right now,' Eve advised Jess.

Jess pulled out her iPhone. 'I'm going to make you appointments too,' she answered. 'It's not going to be any fun if you're not with me.'

Panglet. Again. Because she and Jess wouldn't be doing their first entire prom thing together.

Eve stuck a cheeseburger and a salad on Jess's tray and then on her own as her friend set the appointments. Jess smiled her thanks.

'OK, we're good to go.' Jess returned her phone to her purse. 'I saw the most beautiful pink crystal pendant on bluefly dot com the other night. Do you think it would be crazy to pick the jewellery first and then find the dress to go with it?'

'Pay the nice lady,' Eve told Jess, who was so caught up in what she was saying that she hadn't realized she'd reached the cashier.

'Ooops!' Jess handed over her money. Once Eve had paid too, they walked towards the table where Rose and Jenna were already eating. 'So – crazy to start with a necklace?'

'A challenge, maybe,' Eve replied. 'But there's no wrong way to pick The Dress. You want to start with a necklace as inspiration, why not?'

Jess stopped abruptly, so abruptly that Eve almost ran into her. She turned round and stared at Eve. 'I just realized that you and Luke won't be there. I mean, I knew you wouldn't, but it just hit me. Big time.'

'Well, no. But you'll have an amazing time with

Seth,' Eve said. 'And you and I will do all the girly prep stuff together. So it's good in a way. When it's my turn to go to the prom, we'll get to do all the shopping and primping all over again!' She didn't even get the tiniest of panglets that time. She really did want Jess to have a fabulous prom.

'You and Luke will make one perfect prom picture,' Jess said. 'He's all blond surfer boy and you're all romantic princess with your long dark curls.'

'You think we'll still be together?' Eve asked. 'Senior Prom is three years away for us.'

'Of course,' Jess said with confidence. She lowered her voice. 'The demon babe has tamed the player! Luke is never going to be able to even look at another girl now that he has you.'

Demon babe. How much did Eve love the fact that Jess said that so casually? Just so much. She doubted any of her other friends would be able to accept the fact that Eve was part demon without even blinking, the way Jess had.

Eve hadn't been able to accept it that easily herself. She'd found out the truth when a few drops of her blood had proved fatal to Amunnic, or Many Faces, the latest demon to attack Deepdene. Many Faces had been able to change appearance at will, and fed on the blood of humans – and demon blood was the only way to destroy it. One of the people he'd fed on was Jess's younger brother, Peter. Eve had been able to find him, and most of the demon's other victims, before Many Faces completely drained them. But she'd been too late to save Briony, a new girl at school.

Finding out she was part demon had flipped Eve's world, but knowing that her blood had killed Amunnic and saved lives made her heritage easier to accept. At least for her.

When blood tests done by the Order, an ancient demon-fighting organization, had confirmed that Eve was indeed part demon, it had horrified Callum, one of the Order heads. Eve had seen fear and pity in his eyes the day he'd given her the results of the tests. She could also feel the distrust from Alanna, another member of the Order. It made sense. The Order was founded to hunt down demons. No matter how many demons Eve had killed herself, no one in the Order was ever going to be able to completely trust her.

Eve had gotten used to thinking of herself as the Deepdene Witch, whose mission it was to use her witchy powers to keep her town safe from demons. Amunnic had just been the most recent one she'd had to kill. At first, finding out she was actually one of the things she'd been fighting – part, she reminded her-self, just part – had horrified her as much as it had Callum.

Jess and Luke still trusted her though. They'd helped her get past the fear she'd felt when she learned the truth about herself. They acted like she was the same old Eve. Which she was – the same old power-enhanced Eve.

Who knew? Maybe she'd never have gotten together with Luke if she hadn't been ... *special*. Battling Amunnic side by side had pushed them out of the friend zone and into the couple zone. It had been so intense, and Luke had been staying with her because his dad had been stricken with the plague that warned of Many Faces' arrival, and ... things just happened. Things like kissing. Maybe even things like love – not that either of them had said that word out loud. Yet.

'You two do know that you're blocking traffic?'

A warm flush ran through Eve at the sound of her boyfriend's voice. She turned and grinned at him. 'You can't get round?' she teased.

'I don't want to get round,' he told her. Then he leaned in and gave her a quick kiss.

Life was good. She and Luke were finally together.

She had great friends, a shopping trip to Manhattan in the making, and no demons to deal with!

'I came up with a list of stores that are musts,' Jess told Eve as they stepped out into the warm May afternoon that day after school.

She flipped open her notebook and Eve peered over her shoulder at the list. 'Serendipity sells prom dresses now?' she teased. 'That's so weird for an ice-cream place.'

'We'll need to keep our strength up and stay hydrated,' Jess said innocently. 'Serendipity frozen hot chocolate will take care of that when we're uptown.' She looked up from her notebook and gave a little frown.

'What?' Eve asked.

'I think . . . It looks like Simon Oliver is coming over to us,' Jess murmured.

Simon had had a crush on Jess for about as long as Jess had had a crush on Seth, so in other words, for years and years. For him, the crush just meant staring at Jess a lot, and talking to her even less than he talked to anyone else. Which wasn't much. Simon didn't have any actual friends.

'Us?' Eve followed her friend's gaze. Sure enough,

Simon was walking across the quad on what looked like a collision course with them. Which was weird. Simon said maybe half a dozen words to Eve a semester, and then only if she said something first, but talking to Jess clearly gave him the jitters. It had probably been a year since he'd said a word to her.

'You said hi to him again, didn't you?' Jess joked. 'You got him all *talkative*.'

'I actually did say hi the other day,' Eve admitted. Every once in a while she made the effort. It was just too sad to see him all alone all the time – although maybe that was how he wanted it. 'I don't think he heard me. He was walking down the hall muttering to himself. It didn't even sound like English.'

'Probably Klingon,' Jess suggested. 'Or whatever they speak in World of Warcraft.'

Definite possibility. Simon had a strong geek vibe going and he had the pallor of someone who spent pretty much all his time indoors.

Eve took another quick glance in his direction. He really was coming over to them. She gave a little wave, and he looked at her like he was trying to interpret the strange gesture.

'Um, hi,' he said when he stopped in front of them. Way too close. He always stood too close to people, and he never seemed to realize it. Eve always felt like pulling out that old line from *Dirty Dancing* – '*This is my dance space. This is your dance space.*'

'Hey, Simon,' she said instead.

'I wanted to ask you something, Jess,' he blurted out.

Eve blinked in surprise.

'Sure,' Jess said. 'What's up?' Eve could tell her friend was a little freaked, but Jess was doing her best not to show it. She was always careful not to hurt anyone's feelings.

Simon shifted his backpack – which looked like it contained half the books in the library – from one hand to the other, then shot a look at Eve. 'Alone. If, uh, that's OK,' he added.

Eve glanced at her best friend to make sure she didn't mind being alone with Simon. Jess gave her a quick I'll-be-fine nod. 'I'll wait for you over there,' Eve said, gesturing to one of the stone benches near the huge maple tree on the school lawn.

When she reached the bench, she sat down and rummaged around in her bag for her lip gloss. She didn't want to sit there and stare at Simon and Jess, even though she was kind of curious. Make that *very* curious. Simon and talking – they just didn't go together. Simon and talking to Jess – that went together even less. As far as Eve knew, when Simon wasn't in class, he was in one of the cubbies in the back of the school library, hunched so far over a book that it was hard to see his face.

She applied the vanilla-scented gloss, returned it to her purse, then tilted her head back and closed her eyes, enjoying the feel of the soft, warm breeze brushing over her face. Tonight she and Luke were going to the movies, and Eve tried to decide what she was in the mood for. She wouldn't drag him to a chick flick. She'd wait and go to those with Jess or one of her other girlfriends. Maybe that new horror remake? It could be fun to grab onto Luke and hold on tight. But there'd been enough real-life horror in the past few months. Maybe—

The sound of boys laughing, a bunch of boys, pulled her out of her thoughts. She straightened up and opened her eyes. Jess was coming towards her, Seth at her side, with three of his buds trailing along behind.

Uh-oh. Jess looked mortified. Were they laughing at her? It didn't seem likely. Seth wasn't the kind of guy who'd let his friends give his girlfriend a hard time. Eve stood up. 'What's so funny?' she asked.

Seth and Jess both opened their mouths to answer, but Dave Perry beat them to it. 'Let me tell,' he begged, laughter mixing with his words. 'You're not going to believe this, Eve. That freak just asked Jess if she would "accompany him to the prom". Seriously, that's exactly how he said it. "Accompany him".'

Eve raised her eyebrows, turning to Jess. 'Simon asked you to prom?'

'He didn't know Seth and the guys were behind us,' Jess explained. 'I was just starting to tell him that I'd already been invited when they all went nuts. This one getting all chest-thumpy about me being his girl-friend.' She nudged Seth with her elbow. 'That one laughing until I was afraid he was going to wet him-self.' Jess jerked her thumb towards Dave. 'And the other two very helpfully offering to beat Simon into a hamburger.' She flipped her hand at Al Defrancisco and Connor Bray, who both happened to be on the wrestling team and ended up in scuffles on a regular basis.

Eve sighed and rolled her eyes, and Jess did the same.

'What, you wanted him to ask you?' Seth asked.

'No,' Jess said sharply. She sucked in a breath, and Eve could tell she was trying to get a grip on her temper. 'No,' she said more gently. 'What I wanted was to politely turn him down. Po-lite-ly. You guys were kind of jerks, you know that? You scared him off before I could even say thank you.'

'Oh, kind sir, thank you kindly, but I must refuse your kind offer to escort me to the prom,' Dave said in a high voice and an attempt at what Eve thought was a Southern accent. Al and Connor cracked up. Eve scanned the courtyard for Simon and saw him on the sidewalk just outside the school. He was staring at them.

Eve heart tightened like a fist. The expression on Simon's face was a mix of coldness and fury. His normally pale cheeks had vivid red splotches on them, his mouth was pressed into a hard line, and his eyes glittered as if he had a fever. To Eve it looked like he wanted to come back over and kill Seth and his friends.

Chapter Two

I feel like I'm standing in the power plant again, sucking in all that energy, Eve thought that evening. Back when she was trying to defeat Amunnic, she had discovered that she could do just that: take in electricity and use it to boost her own power, the power she'd inherited as the new Deepdene Witch. Pulling in the electricity had felt amazing, exhilarating, thrilling.

And that's what knowing she had a date with Luke did to her: made her feel all tingly and alive from each strand of hair down to her pinky toes.

'Look at our daughter,' her dad said to her mom. Eve and her parents were just finishing up dinner. 'Does she look odd to you?'

'Odd? I'm not getting a pimple, am I?' Eve exclaimed.

Mr Evergold laughed. 'Nothing like that.' He reached out and gave one of her long, dark ringlets a tweak. 'I was just thinking that you looked almost glittery.'

'As a heart doctor, I'd say the condition is caused by being in love,' Mrs Evergold answered.

Her mother wasn't usually so goofy. That was more a Dad kind of comment. 'I am definitely extremely in *like*,' Eve agreed. Although maybe it was more. Maybe. No guy had ever made her feel the way Luke did. And he was such a cutie with his longish blond hair and those green eyes of his.

'*Extremely in like*,' her father repeated. 'Is that—?'

He was interrupted by the doorbell. 'That's gotta be Luke.' Eve grinned.

'I'll get it. You finish your dinner,' her mom said, rising from the table. A few moments later, she returned with Luke. Eve smiled at him, and decided that her dad had got it right. Glittery was exactly how she felt when she looked at her boyfriend.

'Sit down for a minute,' her father told Luke, and her mother offered him a soda.

'No thanks. I like to get a vat of Sprite at the movies.' He held his hands apart, indicating the world's largest soda cup.

Eve took her last bite of chicken and stood up. 'Just give me one second, and I'll be ready to go,' she told

Luke. She needed to do some quick tooth brushing and lip gloss re-applying.

'I want you two to be sure to stay away from the woods,' her mother said before Eve reached the dining-room door. 'I ran into Becky Poplin at the grocery store. She was putting a flyer up on the bulletin board because their dog – you remember, that little schnauzer? – is lost. There were two other missing pet posters up already, new ones.' She frowned. 'I don't like it. That's a lot of animals in a town this size. It got me wondering if there are still a few of those creatures that killed the Rakoffs' son out in the woods.'

Eve and Luke exchanged a look. They both knew that the creatures – which were actually dog-like demons called wargs – were gone. Helena, the girl who had summoned them, had been a descendant of Lord Medway, the man who had built a portal between our world and hell. He had done it as part of a deal with a demon. The portal allowed the demons into Deepdene, and in exchange they gave him wealth and power.

When Helena learned the truth about her ancestor, she had decided to try to make a pact with a demon herself, but instead, the creatures she'd let through the portal killed her. Eve had used her power to close the portal, preventing the wargs and any other nasties from coming through again. But it wasn't as if she could tell her mother any of that. Parents had a way of not believing in things like demons and hell portals.

'We'll be careful,' Luke told them.

'No going in the woods,' Eve agreed. Still, she couldn't help wondering what had happened to those missing pets since she was positive that the wargs hadn't gotten them.

As Luke walked down Main Street with Eve, he couldn't stop himself glancing over at the woods. The forest surrounded pretty much all of Deepdene, so the treetops were visible from anywhere in the whole town. 'I know we whipped us some warg butt,' he said, 'but the thing your mom was saying about the animals is freaky. Do you think there could be a new demon in Deepdene?'

'Telefriendic moment! I was just thinking the same thing,' Eve exclaimed. 'But I pumped everything I had into closing the portal. Everyone from the Order seemed to think it's secure.'

Luke was glad the Order had made itself available if they needed help with any Deepdene strangeness. He was also glad to have them as an information source. He was working on building a demon data-base. Living in Deepdene, known in its early days as Demondene, he figured it could be useful.

'You're right. They definitely said the portal was shut. Three missing pets doesn't mean that we have to gear up to save the town – again,' he agreed. Although it was normal for him to be a little paranoid. Since he and his dad had moved to Deepdene from Santa Cruz, California, at the beginning of the school year there had been three demon attacks on their new town, one of which had almost killed his father.

'Nope, we can just go to the movies and drink vats of soda like normal teenage people,' Eve answered. She took his hand and swung it back and forth as they walked.

'And maybe after that we can do some of the other things normal teenage people do,' Luke suggested. *Like kissing,* he thought. He loved kissing Eve.

'Possibly. You're thinking homework, right?' Eve teased, her dark blue eyes sparkling.

'Exactly. I was thinking some algebra. Maybe a little social studies,' he shot back, giving her hand a squeeze.

'Look out. Wasp!' Eve exclaimed. He heard a buzz-ing whine, and a second later saw a huge wasp dive-bombing him. He used his free hand to bat it away, but it came right back.

A flash of light – a *pfffft* sound – and the wasp dissolved into ash, the flecks floating away on the slight breeze. 'Taken care of,' Eve said, her voice full of satisfaction.

It had happened so fast that Luke hadn't even realized that the flash was Eve using her powers. In fact, he could still hardly believe it. She'd zapped that thing with her power right on Main Street, which, as usual on a Friday night, was full of people. He glanced around. No one was staring or anything, thank God.

'Nice shot,' Luke said. 'Was that, uh, intentional?' Eve sometimes had trouble controlling her power, especially when she was mad or upset. He'd just brought up the possibility of a new demon in town – and she'd said she'd been thinking about that too. Had that put her on edge?

'You think such precision was an accident?' She smiled up at him.

'I seem to remember a certain innocent jacket that got zapped once,' Luke answered.

'I seem to remember that you got a much more fashionable jacket as a replacement,' Eve replied. 'I've been thinking of giving a few other pieces of your wardrobe a little . . .' She wiggled her fingers.

'As long as I'm not in them, I'll happily take off anything you want me to,' Luke joked. 'But setting my jacket on fire was an accident. At least I thought it was.' He gave her a mock scowl.

'It was, it was. I promise. But I wanted that wasp dead. I hate those little stingy things,' Eve said.

He was a little surprised she'd intentionally used her power against something that was a minor annoyance. But no one wanted to get stung.

'And remember the lasagne I heated up?' she continued. 'That took absolute precision.'

'Why did you have to do that again?' Luke teased. 'Oh right, the power was out. But there wasn't a storm or anything . . . Strange.'

'OK, that was my bad. Although it's good to know I can grab some extra juice if I need to.' They'd been at the power plant that night, and Eve had accidentally taken in so much of the energy surging through the place that she'd blacked out the entire town.

'Absolutely,' Luke agreed. He sat down on the bench in front of the hardware store, pulling her down next to him. They had some time before the movie started. 'So you're not upset about anything?' He had a new thought about what might be bothering her. He hesitated, then lowered his voice and continued. 'You're not still freaked about finding out you're part demon, are you?'

'No,' Eve said quickly. 'I mean, I was. It was hard to get my head around the idea that I have demon blood. I just thought . . . well, I was afraid that having demon blood meant I was evil.'

'You aren't anything close to evil,' Luke assured her. 'A little shallow maybe, a little obsessed with shopping,' he joked, reminding them both of his initial impression of her all those months ago when they first met. 'But you – you're a force for good.'

'It helped so much that you and Jess never doubted me, or acted like I was suddenly something different,' Eve told him. 'But honestly I think what finally made me stop worrying about it was when I found out my great-great-great-grandmother had demon blood too.'

'The old Deepdene Witch,' Luke said. Eve had inherited her powers from her ancestor.

'Yeah. The demon blood is where her power came from – hers and mine. It made me realize that without demon blood, I wouldn't have the strength to fight demons. And who would keep Deepdene safe then?'

She definitely didn't sound upset. Her voice was bright and happy. Luke didn't want to do anything to kill her good mood, but he felt like he had to ask, 'Aren't you afraid that someone might have seen you zap that wasp and wonder about it?'

'It was just a tiny zap. I'm not worried about it,' Eve replied. 'Lately, I'm just loving using my powers. It used to feel like something I had to do because no one else could. Now, it feels like this cool special thing that I'm so lucky I inherited.'

Eve rushed on, her words coming out fast in her enthusiasm. 'Remember that book I found that gave more info on her? It had some amazing stories. Once, she blasted a lake completely dry to kill some kind of aquatic demon that could create tsunamis and hurricanes. And another time she took possession of a demon body and made it eat sugar, because sugar was poisonous to it. She got back out of the body before it died.'

Luke smiled. 'She was like a historical Buffy the Vampire Slayer.'

'Yup. I'm expecting to be starring in my own TV show any day! But I won't forget the little people who knew me way back when.' She knocked his shoulder with hers. 'There could be some great eps based on stuff that my great-great-great did. One time she blasted a demon so hard, she turned it into a human girl. She made it completely harmless. I guess it still had some powers after that, but Granny knocked them so deep they couldn't be reached. The demon could never use them again.'

'I'd watch that,' Luke said. 'Especially if you wore leather pants the way Buffy did.'

'I've noticed something about you,' she answered playfully. 'You never notice fashion unless it involves tight clothes.'

'Or short ones,' Luke added.

Eve shook her head, trying not to smile. 'Anyway, reading about the old Deepdene Witch made me feel even better about being her descendant, demon blood and all. Who knows what *I'll* end up doing? I just feel like I'm ready for anything. Whatever badness comes next – if anything even does – I'm so ready.' Sparks began to crackle from her fingertips. 'Oops!' Eve folded her hands together and the sparks went out.

She was practically giddy with excitement just talking about it. Luke was glad she'd gotten over the revulsion she'd felt when she'd discovered she was part demon. That had been hard to see.

But was she flipping too much the other way? Was

she getting so excited about her powers that she wasn't going to be careful enough with them? She was part demon . . .

That didn't matter. Eve had had the blood the whole time he'd known her. That meant she was the same girl he met back in September. The same completely awesome girl.

The next morning, Eve found herself sitting on the same bench in town where she'd sat with Luke the night before. This time she was waiting for Jess to finish up with her kung fu class. Eve leaned back and tapped on the big window at the front of the hardware store behind the bench. 'Hey, Spiffy,' she called, and the cat inside patted the glass with the pink pads of one paw.

Eve said hi to the kitty pretty much every time she was downtown, and she had since she was a little girl. She was glad to see that Spiffy wasn't one of the currently missing pets.

'Hi-yah!' Jess burst out of the door next to the hardware store, and grinned at Eve. 'Thanks for meeting me. You should have come up and watched for a minute. I am getting to be ridiculously kickass.'

'You always have been,' Eve told her. Jess had been a

cheerleader since the beginning of middle school, and she could jump, flip, kick, cartwheel, all that. But after they found out about Deepdene's demonic history – and Eve's powers – Jess had decided she wanted to learn martial arts. Luke had the demon-killing sword that was given to him by Willem Payne, a high-ranking member of the Order who had died fighting the wargs alongside Eve, Luke and Jess, and Jess wanted to make sure she had something to bring to demon fights too. That's just how Jess was as a friend. If you needed her, she was all in.

'Master Jonah says I'm a natural. He thinks I'll be ready to go for my blue belt by the end of the summer,' Jess said as they started walking towards her house. Luke and Seth were supposed to pick them up there for their mega shopping trip into New York City.

'I tore out a bunch of magazine pictures to give us ideas for your perfect prom dress,' Eve said. 'Not that we don't already have a million ideas ourselves. There's one with these cool off-the-shoulder mesh straps. It has a square neckline, which would really show off that pendant you bought. It might not be The Dress, but the neck and straps are pretty close to perfection.'

'Oooh. Thanks, Evie!' Jess exclaimed. 'Good eye! You're right. The pendant would look great with something like that.'

'Did you have the tux conversation with Seth yet?' Eve asked.

'Uh-huh. I just came out and told him that he had to let me be in charge of what he was wearing. He didn't care,' Jess said.

'He's a guy,' Eve replied with a good-natured shake of her head. 'He's probably relieved that he doesn't have to figure it out himself. Are you going to tell him what kind of corsage to get you?'

'No, that doesn't seem romantic enough,' Jess said.

'Well, no . . .' Eve let her words trail off.

'So I think I'll go with hinting, really obvious hinting,' Jess went on. 'Seth's the best, but he doesn't always pick up on things all that fast.'

'Especially when it's about flowers and not about throwing a ball of some sort.' Seth was on the football and basketball teams at school.

'True that,' Jess agreed.

'On the other hand, he looks very cute when he's throwing a ball of some sort, so who cares if you have to toss him a little suggestion once in a while,' Eve added.

'Very true that!' Jess said. She grabbed Eve's arm. 'Look up there!'

Eve gasped. There was a box on Jess's porch, a blue box with a brown bow.

'MarieBelle,' they exclaimed together. They both j'adored the excessively yummy chocolates, not least because they were so beautiful, with little scenes hand-painted on every one.

'I take it all back, Seth surprises me,' Eve admitted. 'Who knew he – or really any boy – was aware that MarieBelle chocolate is the best ever? Or did you give him one of your *hints*?'

'I didn't. Not even a teeny one,' Jess answered, picking up the box and hugging it to her chest. 'This is so sweet of him.' She giggled. 'Sweet.'

'Absolutely sweet,' Eve agreed, wondering if Luke would ever do something ultra-romantic, like surprise her with a special gift.

'I already know which one you want.' Jess untied the ribbon, and a card in a heavy cream envelope fell free. She opened it carefully, and managed not to make even a tiny tear. Eve knew the card would go into what Jess called her treasure box, a hatbox where she kept mementoes of her favourite moments.

'Are you going to tell me what it says, or are you

going to start keeping secrets from your bestie?' Eve asked. Jess didn't answer. 'What's wrong? You're all pale.'

'It's not from Seth,' Jess told her.

'Someone's trying to steal you away?' Eve exclaimed. 'Who?'

Jess stared at the card a moment longer, then raised her eyes to Eve. 'They're from Simon. Don't you think that's kind of, I don't know . . .' She shrugged.

Eve frowned. 'I actually thought it was brave of him to ask you to the prom yesterday. You know how he's been crushing on you for *ever*. It might have been the first time he's ever asked a girl out. At least we've never seen him out with anyone. Asking you, awesome you, to the biggest event of the year, that took real courage,' she said. 'But you said no. And Seth made it really clear you're with him. I don't get why Simon would do this.'

'Maybe he ordered the chocolates before he asked me,' Jess suggested, wrapping the brown ribbon around her wrist over and over.

'But they were hand-delivered. MarieBelle doesn't have a delivery service,' Eve pointed out. 'Simon must have brought them over himself, which means he still brought them even though you'd turned him down.'

She flashed back on Simon's expression as he looked at Seth and his friends yesterday afternoon. He'd looked humiliated and furious at the same time. Had he been so angry that he was going to keep coming after Jess to prove some kind of point? She decided not to mention that theory to Jess. She wanted her friend to be able to hang onto her prom high.

'Maybe you're right, though,' Eve said. 'Maybe he'd already gotten the chocolates and decided just to give them to you since he had them. What did he say in the card anyway?'

Jess wrinkled her nose. '"Yours always." That's just wrong and weird.'

'Well, Simon isn't exactly known for having good social skills. He probably read some blog that gave him the idea,' Eve commented. 'Now, come on. You know I'm waiting for my white kona coffee bean one.'

'You think it's OK to eat them? It feels kind of bad when we've just been saying how clueless and weird he is,' Jess said.

'I said he was brave, so I definitely get one,' Eve said. 'And you were nice to him yesterday. Not everyone would have been. I think it's just good karma coming around. And don't you just love when good karma comes in the form of chocolate?'

'We're not letting Peter see these,' Jess said as she led the way into the house. 'My little brother doesn't deserve any, because he has no appreciation of good chocolate. He'd be as happy with a jumbo bag of M&Ms.'

'And the way he inhales food, I'm not sure he's even able to taste it,' Eve said. But she smiled. Peter was basically her honorary little brother, and most of the things he did that annoyed Jess just made Eve laugh. She didn't even mind the way he teased her non-stop and called her 'Evie-weevie'.

She was so glad he'd gotten over seeing her use her powers against Amunnic. It had scared him. Badly. He'd had a hard time even looking at her for weeks. Finally, just a couple of days ago, he'd started acting like his usual self, and Eve was very relieved.

Before they even reached the living room, Eve heard Peter walking along the landing. It had to be him. Neither of Jess's parents made that kind of noise.

Jess tried to hide the box of candy behind her back, but she was too slow. 'I know you got chocolate. Don't even try to deny it,' Peter yelled as he started thundering down the stairs. 'Give me some.'

'I think he could have one. Just one,' Eve said, hoping she might score a few points with him. Even

36

though he was almost totally normal around her, she knew he'd never forget seeing her use her powers. And lightning bolts shooting from the fingers – that could be a terrifying sight, even if those bolts were killing a blood-drinking demon.

'Evie-weevie! Always got my back!' Peter held a hand up for a high-five when he reached her, and Eve slapped his palm. 'So what are we doing? What's the plan for the afternoon?'

'We – as in me and Eve – are in prom-countdown mode,' Jess told her brother. 'We're going to Manhattan to shop.' She opened the box of chocolates and held it out to her best friend. Eve picked out her favourite flavour and took a nibble. She smiled as Peter began making little whining puppy sounds. He was such a goof.

'You can have one, as in *one*.' Jess held up one finger, then offered the chocolates to Peter.

Peter grabbed one of the beautifully painted chocolates and stuffed the whole thing in his mouth. 'So, let me help with the prom-shopping stuff. I can give the man's opinion.'

'Did you just call yourself a man?' Eve teased, happy that Peter was teasable again.

'He's just trying to get more chocolate,' Jess said.

She gave an exaggerated sigh. 'Take one more, then go back to your man-cave. Luke and Seth are coming shopping with us. They'll provide all the testosterone we need.'

Peter grabbed another chocolate and popped it in his mouth, even though Eve suspected he hadn't finished eating the first. 'You know where to find me when you realize no one will tell you the truth about how you look in those dresses the way I will,' he said as he started back up the stairs. 'You can rely on me to always say if something makes your butt look big,' he called over his shoulder.

Eve stared after him. 'It seems like he's really getting over the Amunnic thing. What he saw me do.'

'I told you he would,' Jess answered. 'He just needed a little time. The whole Many Faces thing really shook him up. At least the other victims seem to have forgotten everything.'

'All that blood loss. And the shock.' Eve turned to Jess. 'You don't know how good it felt to hear him call me "Evie-weevie".'

'You're disturbed, you know that?' Jess joked.

Eve nodded happily, feeling extra glad they hadn't told Peter that she was part demon. He'd never have gotten over that. Never.

Chapter Three

Jess took one last look in the mirror, then headed out of her bedroom. She'd left Eve downstairs while she showered the kung fu sweat off her in case the guys showed up early.

Whee! I'm about to go shopping for The Dress! She gave a little twirl as she started down the hall. She kept doing that. Twirling. She couldn't help it. She didn't think she'd ever been so happy. But she'd never been going to the Senior Prom with Seth before – Seth who she'd been crushing on for ever! She felt like someone had taken a Bedazzler to her – but not tacky, just sparkly.

She hesitated at the doorway, then turned and grabbed the box of chocolates off her dresser. Somehow she didn't want them in her room. And it wasn't like she could offer any to Seth.

Jess hurried down the hall, then stopped at Peter's room and gave a couple of quick knocks.

'I knew you'd realize you needed me!' he said as he swung open the door.

'What I need you for is eating the rest of these.' She thrust the box of chocolates at him. 'I so don't want a volcanic pimple erupting just in time for the prom, and you don't have anything you have to look good for,' she added with a smile.

'No, I don't,' he agreed happily, popping two more chocolates into his mouth.

'I'm glad you've gotten over being weirded out about Eve,' she told him, keeping her voice low, even though Eve shouldn't be able to hear her from downstairs. 'I know what you saw . . . it looked horrible.'

'But it saved my life. And everybody else's,' Peter said. 'For a while I guess that whole day was one big glob of badness, and Eve seemed as bad as everything else, firing out those lightning bolts.'

'It really hurt Eve that you started acting all freaked around her,' Jess answered. 'I understood why, and I tried to explain it to her.'

'Truth? I'm still a little freaked,' Peter admitted. 'It's hard to look at her and just see . . . Eve. The old Eve. I'm trying though. I *do* know I wouldn't even be standing here if it wasn't for her.'

'I'm proud of you.' Jess didn't think she'd ever said

that to him before, but she meant it. 'You should have seen how happy she was that you were being your usual obnoxious self around her.'

'Cool.' Peter's brows drew together. 'She is the same, right? I mean, you know her better than anyone. If she was different, you'd be the one to see it.'

'You don't have to worry,' Jess promised. 'Eve is Eve. She's just a little new and improved – now with demon-killing power.' *And demon blood*, not that she'd ever tell Peter that.

Peter nodded. 'Yeah. But isn't it weird that there weren't any demons here until Eve got that power? It kind of seems like she's almost a demon magnet. And that means whoever's around her is going to keep getting attacked. Just . . . be careful when you're with her, OK?'

Awww. Her little brother was worried about her. That was so sweet. 'Why do you think I've been taking kung fu? I know I need to be ready for anything.' She wasn't going to let Eve protect the town all by herself. Eve had power, but that didn't mean she didn't need Jess and Luke backing her up. Jess smiled at her brother and headed for the stairs. 'Try to show some self-control with that candy,' she called back. 'You'll get sick if you eat it all in one day.'

She was still thinking about the candy when she reached the living room and plopped down on the sofa next to Eve. 'I think I have to call Simon.'

Eve nodded. 'He needs to know that you're with Seth and that he shouldn't be sending you presents.'

'Although how can he not know that after the way Seth and his boys acted yesterday?' Jess asked. 'Oh, well. At least this time I can be polite, like I wanted to be. I didn't even manage to say thank you to him after he asked me.'

'Which so wasn't your fault,' Eve told her.

'Come with me. I need moral support.' Jess led the way to the kitchen, looked up Simon's number in the school directory her mom kept in the junk drawer, then phoned him before she could change her mind.

Simon picked up.

'Hi. Um. It's Jess. Jess Meredith,' Jess said uncertainly.

'Jess! Hello!' He sounded really excited. Nervous too. His voice had a little quaver in it.

'Hi, Simon. I wanted to say thank you for asking me to the prom, and for the chocolates. They're so beautiful I can hardly make myself eat them,' Jess began. 'But, here's the thing, I've been going out with Seth for a while now. He's my boyfriend, so . . .'

Jess paused, waiting for an answer. But Simon didn't say anything. She hoped she hadn't hurt his feelings. She'd chosen every word carefully.

The silence continued, and Jess shot a nervous glance at Eve. Did she really have to spell it out more? Eve gave her an encouraging pat on the hand, and leaned close so she'd be able to hear if Simon said anything. He didn't. The silence stretched out, and out, and out. Jess couldn't take it any more. 'Anyway, like I said, I wanted to tell you thanks. But I'm not available.'

Available? Had she really just used that word?

Simon uttered several harsh, guttural sounds, then hung up. Jess stared at the phone, confused. 'Did he say something?' she asked Eve.

'It kind of sounded like what he was muttering in the hall the other day,' Eve replied, her brows pulling together in a frown.

'Well, now that I've heard it myself, I don't think it's Klingon or World of Warcraft or any other kind of geekspeak,' Jess said. Whatever it had been, it had given her the creeps. She was glad she hadn't understood the strange words. The way he'd said them made it clear that they didn't mean anything good.

* * *

'It sounds like you have a big admirer, Jess,' Luke said. Jess had just finished telling the guys about the candy and the phone call. 'Or should I stay stalker?'

Seth gave a snort. 'Stalker sounds way too menacing for Simon. He can hardly look at a girl without his knees knocking.'

'Just try to make the sounds he made,' Luke told Eve and Jess. 'Maybe we can figure out what he meant.'

'What does it matter?' Eve asked. The four of them were walking towards the station to head for the city. They shouldn't be talking about Simon when they were starting on their fabulous jaunt to Manhattan.

'Was it something like . . .' Luke made a sound that started out sort of like a rooster and segued into a kind of elephant trumpet.

'I can't remember the sounds well enough to make them,' Jess said, speaking loudly to be heard over Luke.

'Me neither,' Eve said. 'So can we please have a subject change?'

'Sure,' Luke said. 'What do you want to discuss? Global climate change? Strategies to end homelessness? How to achieve world peace?' He winked at Eve.

'You don't think I could talk about any of those

things, but I could,' Eve told him.

'I just still can't believe that guy had the nerve to give you chocolates after it should have been clear that we're together,' Seth said.

'It's over now. I told him how things were, and that's it,' Jess assured him, slipping one arm around his waist.

Eve caught a flash of movement out of the corner of her eye. She spun towards it, just in time to see a basketball bouncing off Seth's back.

Seth grabbed it, twirled it on one finger, then threw it back at Connor, who stood about half a block behind them, laughing his head off. And getting annoyed glances from a couple of Main Street shoppers.

'We're getting a game up over at the Y. You two in?' he shouted to Luke and Seth.

'Nope,' Jess called back. 'These boys are ours for the entire day.' She made a flicking motion with her hands. 'You go play,' she teased.

Connor dribbled the ball a few times. 'Your loss,' he said.

They started walking again. 'Where are you all off to?' Jess's neighbour Megan Christie, who was also at Deepdene High, was now heading across the road towards them. On Main Street you could easily see half the people you knew in about half an hour.

Eve heard Jess give a little sigh and knew she was relieved to have another distraction from the subject of Simon. 'We're doing a shop-till-you-drop,' she answered.

'With boys? You know they'll drop hours and hours and hours before you and Eve do?' Megan said.

'Hey, we're athletes,' Luke protested. 'We aren't going to have a problem walking through some stores.'

Megan shook her head, making a little clucking sound with her tongue. '"Walking through some stores",' she repeated. 'Clearly you've never been shopping with these two.'

'What do you have going today?' Jess asked her.

'Even though I'm older than you, I, sadly, don't yet have a prom dress to buy.' She didn't sound too upset. There was no doubt Megan, one of the flirtiest, most popular girls in school, would be going to her prom when she was a senior. 'I'm meeting up with Shanna and Elisa. We're seeing that dying-girl movie.' She pulled a mini-pack of Kleenex decorated with hearts out of her purse. 'I'm prepared.'

'I want to see that too. You have to tell me what it's like,' Eve said.

'Will do. And you two' – she pointed from Luke to Seth – 'on Monday I expect you to report in on whether football, basketball, or shopping is more gruelling.' She waved and started back across the street.

'On the subject of shopping, how do you all feel about making a quick stop in East Hampton?' Jess asked. 'When I was taking a shower, I remembered that I'd seen this gorgeous dress in the window of the Cynthia Rowley boutique. I need to look at it again, so I can compare and contrast.'

'Fine by me,' Seth answered.

'Me too,' Luke put in. 'Do you think we need to stretch first?' he asked Seth. 'We don't want to pull a muscle.'

'You know how girls always say that one of the things they look for in a guy is a sense of humour?' Eve asked. When Luke nodded, grinning, she continued, 'That's not my thing.' He just grinned wider.

'So East Hampton it is,' Jess said.

'Absolutely. If you don't look at the dress now, it'll get more and more gorgeous in your mind, and you won't like anything else we see,' Eve answered. 'But then when you go look at it later, it could actually not be especially gorgeous at all.'

'Exactly!' Jess smiled at her.

'And that's why we're taking pics of all the possibilities,' Eve reminded her.

'Want to cut through the woods?' Seth asked. 'It's not a bad walk to East Hampton. We can be there in about fifteen minutes.'

Eve and Luke exchanged a glance. She knew he was thinking about the missing animals. So was she. But the portal was closed, and if somehow something nasty had gotten into the woods, she could handle it. Before she met Jess that morning, she'd made a quick stop at the power plant. The energy was still churning inside her, and it would love to get out. Not that she wanted anything bad to happen, of course. It was just nice to feel powerful and prepared.

'I'm up for a walk in the woods,' Eve said. *Why not check things out?* she thought. Jess and Luke agreed, and a few minutes later they were entering the cool darkness of the trees. Eve hadn't been there since she, Jess and Luke had battled the wargs. That night, she'd seen a dead body for the first time, the body of Willem Payne, the Order member who had battled the demons alongside them. The memory made her shiver.

She told herself not to think about that night, not

now. 'So, Seth, I heard that you've given Jess full control of picking your tux. Smart move.'

'Oh, I forgot to tell you,' Seth said, turning to Jess. 'My dad still has the tux he wore to his prom. He said I could borrow it.'

Jess rolled her eyes. 'That was when, the early eighties?' she asked.

'Something like that.' Seth shrugged.

'I'm picturing a pastel suit. I'm picturing a gigantic floppy bow tie and a shiny matching cummerbund. What I'm not picturing is going to the prom with a guy dressed like that. *Ewww!*' Jess squealed.

'Relax. I was just kidding,' Seth told her.

Jess didn't respond. She was staring down at the ground. Slowly she lifted her foot. A gasp escaped from Eve's throat. The bottom of Jess's loafer was smeared with gore. 'Oh, God. I stepped on a dead squirrel,' Jess cried. She began frantically scraping her shoe against a tree trunk, trying to wipe off the blood.

'Here. Give it to me.' Seth held out his hand for the shoe. Once Jess gave it to him, he used some leaves to clean it for her, then put it back on her foot, all Prince Charming.

Luke crouched down and studied the body of the small animal. He frowned and shot a worried look at

Eve. She forced herself to study the squirrel more closely. Almost immediately she saw what was bothering Luke. There were no teeth marks or claw marks on the squirrel's body, nothing that indicated an attack by another animal. Its throat had been neatly slit.

'Looks like some kid found it and messed around with it after it died,' Seth suggested. He'd clearly come to the same conclusion about the wound as Eve had: that it certainly hadn't been made by an animal. 'I got a Swiss Army knife when I was eleven, and I tried it out on everything.' Jess shot him a horrified glance, and he quickly added, 'I never did anything like this, though. It was more like I'd try to cut through a soda can, that kind of thing.'

Jess whipped her head towards Eve. 'What if it was killed by what killed Kyle!' she exclaimed. 'Could that animal be back?' Her voice got higher with the question. She knew exactly what *that animal* had been.

'Of course it can't. There haven't been any attacks for months. Those science experts said it had moved on,' Seth said.

'I think they're right. Even if it was one of those animals – remember some people thought it was a pack – it would have to be feeding, and that would leave evidence,' Luke added.

Eve nodded. 'They have to be far away,' she told Jess, saying the words slowly and deliberately, so that Jess would get the message – the wargs were still trapped on the other side of the portal, and the portal was closed. There was no way they could be back in Deepdene. She was glad she hadn't told Jess about the missing animals her mother mentioned the other night. Jess would be even more scared right now – and she looked pretty scared already.

'Like I said, if the animal was back, there'd be evidence of it feeding,' Luke assured her. 'One dead squirrel, that's definitely not evidence. They wouldn't go after something so small. And anyway, there's no sign of anyone having tried to eat this thing.'

Eve could see that her friend was convinced now. She was convinced too. But, still, the woods seemed a little darker, even though she knew the light hadn't actually changed. 'So,' she said. 'Tell us what you have planned for Seth on prom night. We know it won't be a pastel tuxedo.'

She knew exactly what kind of tux Jess had in mind, of course. But talking about the prom would make Jess happy and take her mind off the squirrel. It would also make the woods feel more normal.

'It all depends on the dress, obviously,' Jess

answered, the smile returning to her face. 'But definitely single-breasted, probably three or four buttons.' Luke and Seth exchanged a who-knows-what-she's-talking-about-but-whatever look. Jess didn't notice, just kept talking. 'Those look great on tall guys, and—'

'Watch your step,' Luke called. 'Up ahead, another squirrel.'

Eve took a long look. There was a slit along the squirrel's throat. A warg wouldn't have left anything but a few specks of blood and flesh behind if it had bothered to attack something so small. This wound obviously hadn't been made by some ordinary animal. That meant the squirrels had been killed by a human – or a demon. She knew by now that there were many different types of demon. Maybe one had used a knife to kill. Or had a single sharp claw, or something.

'Come on. Let's walk faster. I'm ready to get out of the woods and into the stores.' Jess picked up the pace. Luke grabbed Eve's hand as they followed her.

'I should have brought a sweater,' Eve commented. 'I was fine when we were out in the sun, but it's a lot colder in the woods.'

'You think so?' Jess asked. 'I didn't notice.'

'I didn't notice at first either. It just hit me,' Eve said. Luke let go of her hand and wrapped his arm around her shoulders.

'You *are* cold! You've got goose bumps,' he exclaimed. He rubbed his hand up and down her bare arm.

Eve nodded. She did. Not just on her arms, either. Her whole body was covered. That had never happened before. She felt cold inside too, like she'd been eating ice. Her lungs felt frozen, unable to expand enough to bring in air.

Eve reached out and put her hand on a tree trunk, leaning most of her weight on it as she struggled for breath. 'Hold up,' Luke called to Jess and Seth. 'There's something wrong with Eve.'

'I've got to go back,' Eve managed to say through chattering teeth. She'd thought being so cold your teeth chattered was limited to freezing winter nights, but hers were clicking together uncontrollably even though it was May. 'I need to get in bed under a blanket.'

'I'll get you back.' Luke tightened his hold on her shoulders. 'Lean on me.' He helped her turn round and she was able to take a few shaky steps. Jess and Seth stayed close behind them. Eve was scared; she wasn't sure she'd be able to make it out of the woods even with Luke supporting her, but as they retraced their steps, she began to be able to pull in deep breaths of the warm spring air.

'That was weird.' The words came out clearly. Her teeth had stopped chattering. 'I felt like I couldn't breathe.'

'It wasn't just weird, it was scary,' Jess said. 'You went really pale, Eve.'

'You're OK now?' Luke asked, his eyes dark with worry.

Eve nodded. 'Still sort of cold, but OK.' She stopped walking, and forced a smile at her friends. 'I still want to go home, though. Jess, you and the boys go shop. I know they won't be any real help, but they can carry things. And you can text me dress pictures.'

'No way. I am not shopping for my prom dress without you,' Jess replied. 'Just not happening. We can go tomorrow if you're feeling better.'

'If you think I'm going to let you walk home alone after what just happened, you're crazy,' Luke added.

'Skipping the trip is fine by me,' Seth said. 'I hate shopping.'

'Let's go back to my place. It's closer,' Jess suggested as they continued walking out of the woods, and Eve and the guys agreed right away. With each step, Eve felt better.

What was *that?* she wondered as they reached the edge of the woods and stepped out onto the sidewalk. The sunlight streaming down on her felt as good as a cashmere sweater. *That was so freaky, the way it came and went in seconds.*

'You still feeling all right?' Luke asked. 'I can call my dad for a ride.'

He was such a good guy. 'I'm fine. Really,' Eve told him. 'More than fine.' She proved it by keeping up her end of a lively discussion about what everybody had planned for the summer. It lasted all the way to Jess's.

'Uh-oh.' Jess stopped in front of her mailbox. A thick cream-coloured envelope was poking out. It looked just like the one that had come with the candy. 'No address. Somebody has hand-delivered it.' She glanced at Eve, and Eve knew they were thinking the same thing. Simon had been back.

Jess ripped open the envelope, not bothering to open it carefully as she had with the previous one. There was no chance this was going in her memory hatbox.

'What is it?' Seth asked.

'It's from Simon,' Jess told him.

Seth cursed under his breath. 'That guy is out of control. What does it say?'

Jess began to read as they walked up the flagstone path to her house. 'He says that he didn't think I was the type of person to judge someone by appearances, but clearly he was wrong about me. Then he calls me cold and callous.'

'That is so not you,' Eve cried. 'You're toasty warm and well-moisturized. You—' She forgot what she was about to say as her eyes snagged on a few droplets of glistening red shining up from one of the stones of the Merediths' walkway. For a moment Eve thought it was nail polish. Then she saw a bigger puddle near the bushes that ran under the living-room window. *Blood*, she realized. It was blood. It looked so wrong against the perfectly manicured green of the lawn.

Eve's breath caught in her chest. Was there a new demon on the loose? Was it still around? The last thing they needed was to have Seth see her use her powers.

Jess saw the blood a second later, and let out a shriek. Then another, high and shrill and horrible to hear. Her father burst out the front door. 'Jess! What's happened?'

She pressed her fingers to her lips, unable to answer.

'Over here,' Eve told him. She walked across to the bushes, scanning the area for any sign that a demon was nearby. Luke remained at her side. So did Mr Meredith. Seth hung back with Jess. Eve could hear him murmuring reassurances as she crouched down on the balls of her feet to get a closer look. She began breathing through her mouth to avoid the familiar – way too familiar – metallic smell of fresh blood.

'It looks like a cat,' Jess's dad said. He pushed a clump of the bushes aside. 'Yeah, that's what it is. I think it's Pumpkin from down the street.'

'His throat has been slit,' Luke observed. His hand moved reflexively to his back, and Eve knew he was wishing he had the demon-killing sword strapped under his shirt the way he did when they were sure a demon was on the loose.

'We saw a couple of squirrels that had been killed like that, out in the woods,' Eve added, wishing she could reach over and close Pumpkin's staring golden eyes. 'Do you think something could have followed us back?' she asked Luke, knowing he'd understand she meant a demon.

'Pumpkin was dead when we got here,' he reminded her. 'That means whatever killed him was here before we showed up. It's probably gone now.' But Eve could see that the muscles in his jaw were tense, and his hands had curled into fists.

'The poor thing must have been killed right near here,' Mr Meredith said thoughtfully. 'There wouldn't be so much blood if he hadn't. And you're right about the wound, Luke. It looks like the throat was deliberately slit. Another animal couldn't have done this. Someone stood right in front of the house and . . .' His words trailed off and he shook his head. He released the clump of bush, and it sprang back into place. 'I'm going to go get something to wrap him in.'

Eve stood up, but she and Luke didn't move. It was as if the blood had cast a spell on them. Neither could look away.

'Why would this animal-killer risk coming so close to Jess's house?' Eve murmured. She didn't want to say the word 'demon' aloud, not with Mr Meredith and Seth nearby. She shot a look over her shoulder at her friend. Seth had managed to calm Jess down, at least a little.

'You said that Jess called Simon just before we left, right?' Luke asked.

'Pretty much,' Eve said. 'Maybe five minutes before.'

'And he sounded angry,' Luke continued.

'Definitely, even though we didn't understand what

he actually said,' Eve agreed. 'You don't think . . . Do you think he was angry enough to kill the cat? He could have thought he was Jess's. Pumpkin wanders over here a lot.' She was relieved that there was an explanation other than a demon in their town. But the idea that Simon could have done something so violent was almost as frightening.

Luke sighed. 'I don't know. It's something to think about,' he said. 'But there are the squirrels too. And I'm really starting to wonder what happened to those missing pets your mom told us about.'

'I don't understand it,' Mr Meredith said when he returned with a towel. 'Just this morning, I was golfing with a friend, and he said he'd seen a dead dog in the middle of the road when he was driving back into town last night. He mentioned it because the dog hadn't been hit by a car. He said it looked like its throat had been cut with a knife.'

Chapter Four

That night Eve sat propped up in her bed, wearing the Santa Cruz T-shirt Luke had given her. She loved sleeping in it; it was so oversized and comfy. And it still had a little of that yummy Luke smell.

She clicked the remote, but nothing on the TV could hold her attention. Her mind was doing some channel-surfing of its own, flashing images – all of them unpleasant. Dead squirrel, dead squirrel, dead kitty, Jess's scared face, blood on the lawn, and Eve herself, standing paralysed in the woods, her entire body coated with ice. Not that that's exactly what had happened, but that's what her brain was showing, probably because that's what it had felt like to Eve. She'd felt like she was encased in ice.

You're fine, Eve told herself. And she was. There were still no after-effects from that moment in the woods.

Still, maybe she'd stop by the power plant in the morning before she met up with Jess. A smile tugged at her lips as an idea occurred to her. There was no reason for her to wait until tomorrow. She could juice up a little right now, right here.

She reached over and slipped her hand under the shade of the lamp on her bedside table. The light bulb went out with a soft pop, and Eve felt a corresponding pop inside her, a little pop of new power.

Nice. But more would be nicer. Especially with the possibility that a demon was in Deepdene.

Eve scrambled to the edge of her bed, leaned forward, and pressed both hands against the large screen of her TV. With a crackle, it went out, and Eve instantly felt that power joining the hot core inside her.

She glanced around the room. What else?

She realized she'd been kind of destructive. All she'd been thinking about was the power. She didn't want to ruin her computer or her CD player or anything else. But why not go right to the source?

Would it even work? Eve didn't know. But she slid off the bed and sat cross-legged in front of one of the power outlets. Gently she pressed two fingers against the slots for a plug. She couldn't stop herself from giggling as the hot electric sizzle zipped up her fingers and zigzagged through her entire body.

'If you're out there, demon-breath, bring it on,' she whispered. Right before the overhead light went out.

'Why is the power out again?' her mother exclaimed. 'This seems to happen every week!'

'Maybe someone ran their car into an electric pylon,' Eve heard her dad suggest.

'I'll go get the candles,' Eve called to them. Not that she really needed them. If she wanted to, she was pretty sure she could light up the whole town.

'I hope they still have that dress at Cynthia Rowley,' Jess said on Sunday.

'If they don't, it's not meant to be,' Eve told her. 'We must trust the prom gods.' She and Jess were walking down Main Street. Neither of the guys were available for shopping that afternoon, so they'd decided to make the jaunt to East Hampton to check on the possibly perfect prom dress Jess had seen.

'Are you sure you want to go through the woods after what happened yesterday?' Jess asked. 'You felt pretty sick, and those squirrels are probably still there. We could just hop on the train.'

'No, I'm up for walking. That *was* pretty bizarre

yesterday, but I feel fine now,' Eve assured her. 'In fact, I felt better almost right away, and whatever it was never came back.' She spotted something white and floaty out of the corner of her eye and whirled towards it. A soft 'oooh' escaped her lips as she took in the phenomenally gorgeous dress in the window of the Dolce & Gabbana boutique. Strapless, form-fitting until the knees, where it flared into a cascade of chiffon layers that went to the floor with just a few ruffles. Romantic, classy, a little bit princess, and just so, so Eve. 'Dibbies!' she cried, pointing to it.

Eve and Jess had created the *dibbies* system years ago. It made shopping together much more fun and much less stressful, because there were always things they both liked and both wanted, but it's not like they could buy matching clothes. That would be ridiculous. So they each got to call 'dibbies' on three items per shopping trip. Calling 'dibbies' meant the caller had first shot at whatever the item was – in this case the most insanely beautiful dress Eve had ever seen. She could already imagine the besotted expression on Luke's face when he saw her in it.

Jess didn't say anything, which was seriously unusual for Jess. Eve glanced over and saw her best friend staring at the dress with lust and longing all over her face. 'You were too slow, missy. You need some dibbies practice,' Eve teased her. 'I can't wait to try it on! What do you think for shoes? Maybe a nude high-heeled sandal.' She opened the door of the boutique and stepped inside, holding it open for Jess. 'Nothing that takes attention away from the dress, I don't think.'

But Jess was still standing in the same spot. She hadn't moved even an inch towards the door. It was like she'd grown roots.

'Come on. Maybe you'll find something in here too,' Eve said. They'd obviously gotten a bunch of new stuff in – like the gorgeous dress. If it had been there before, Eve would have noticed it. It pulled her like a magnet.

'Eve . . . we're shopping for *my* prom dress. Why are you calling dibbies?' Jess asked, her tone just a little whiny, which wasn't like her.

'Well, we're mainly shopping for you, but that doesn't mean I don't get to buy anything, does it?' Eve asked. 'You wouldn't torture me like that.'

Jess still didn't move to the door Eve was holding open. 'Of course not. You can shop, but . . .' She hesitated, then looked at the dress again.

Eve got it. 'You like it too, right?'

'Love it,' Jess answered. 'Love it, love it, love it.'

This was exactly the situation dibbies had been created for. With dibbies there was no fighting, no tears. Whoever called it first got first chance to buy. That was law. 'I'm sure we'll see tons of great dresses. If not today, then when we make our big shopping expedition to the city.' They were going to wait and go to Manhattan when the boys could go with them.

'It's a prom dress, though,' Jess said. 'And you're not going to the prom. You don't even have anyplace to wear it.'

Eve felt a pang – a full pang, not just a panglet. What Jess had said really stung. Didn't she understand how hard it was to see her going off to the prom when they'd always planned on double dating?

'I was thinking I'd wear it to the HEART charity event,' Eve said, trying to hide her hurt.

'You can't wear a gown on the beach,' Jess protested. 'You'd ruin it.'

Eve felt a little stunned. Dibbies was law. But being a true best friend was even more important, she told herself. Jess was clearly smitten with the dress, and she did have the absolute perfect place to wear it. Dibbies or no, Eve wasn't going to try to take the dress away. Eve smiled. It was a little hard to make her lips turn up, but only a little. 'Dibbies withdrawn. That might just be The Dress,' she told Jess. 'Can you see it with the pendant you liked?'

Jess finally walked through the door, and Eve let it swing closed behind them. 'It would be perfect,' Jess replied. 'Better than perfect.'

'Go grab it and try it on before some other prom girl spots it,' Eve advised her.

'I will.' Jess rushed towards the sales assistant, and disappeared into a changing room a few moments later.

Eve walked to the nearest rack and began flipping through what turned out to be bathing suits. Truly, a girl could never have too many bathing suits, especially with a pool in the backyard and the beach a few blocks away. But none of the bright little slips of cloth grabbed her attention. She kept thinking about how she'd look in the dress Jess was trying on right that second as she clicked though the hangers faster and faster.

She heard a hiss, a crackle, then sparks jumped off the rack. 'What—' the assistant exclaimed.

Eve jerked her hand away from the hangers quickly.

'You should get someone to look at that,' she cried. 'It gave me a shock.'

'I will,' the woman assured her. She shook her head. 'I've never seen anything like that.'

Eve moved away, on to another rack, this one of sheer, summery dresses. She looked at them, but didn't trust herself to touch the hangers. Her power had come out so fast, so unexpectedly. She couldn't risk that happening again. She didn't—

'Opinion?' Jess called softly, pulling Eve away from her thoughts.

Eve turned and faced her. 'Gorgeous,' she said, with absolute honesty. The dress clung and flowed in all the right places, the neckline showing off just the right amount of cleavage. 'Fairy princess meets prom queen.' She pulled her iPhone out of her bag. 'Let me get a picture. Do you think you'll wear your hair up for the prom?'

'Probably,' Jess answered. She quickly twisted her hair into a knot on the top of her head and Eve took several pics.

'You're sure it's OK if I decide to get it? You did call it,' Jess said.

'Of course I'm sure,' Eve told her. 'It's the Senior Prom we're talking about.'

Jess rushed over and gave her a hard hug. 'Thanks. You're the best.' She started back towards the dressing room.

I'm the best, Eve told herself.

Why didn't that make her feel better?

'Tell me if you see anything dead, especially dead and squishy,' Jess said as they walked through the woods on their way to East Hampton. She'd been giving Eve the same instruction almost every fifteen metres the entire time, and Eve was relieved that they were almost there. 'I don't want to have to throw away these shoes too. I thought about buying a pair of Crocs just for walking through the woods, but even the possibility of slimy ickiness could not get me into plastic shoes.'

'Still no dead squishiness. Or slimy ickiness,' Eve replied. 'No squirrels, nothing.'

'I'm so glad they let me put the dress on hold,' Jess said. She still wanted to take another look at the possibly extremely gorgeous dress she'd seen in East Hampton, even though when she'd tried on the Dolce & Gabbana gown it had looked as if it had been made with her body in mind.

I'm not sure she really loves, loves, loves the dress, at

least not the way I do, Eve thought, *or she would have bought it on the spot.*

'I know, that's great!' she said out loud, pushing down her sadness. She was going to be happy for her friend. That's all there was to it. 'So what's this Cynthia Rowley dress like? Or should I not know, so I can give you my gut first impression?'

'It's white, with grey rosettes under the bust and then just one circle of them around the dress further down, at an angle. Grey isn't a colour I'd usually think of for prom, but there's just a little bit of it.'

'Sounds sophisticated, and I bet the pink pendant would look really good with it,' Eve said.

'Are you OK?' Jess asked.

'Mmm-hmm. Why?' Eve replied.

'You're walking slowly,' Jess pointed out. 'It's like you suddenly stepped into a pool of quicksand.'

It was true. Eve hadn't noticed right away, but her feet felt heavier. As she continued walking, they got heavier and heavier with each step. She began panting with the effort, but the air was so cold it was like the oxygen had frozen and wasn't available to her body. She shivered.

'Eve!' Jess cried. 'It's happening again. You're all goose-bumpy.'

Eve didn't have enough breath to answer. She took one more step, then her knees buckled and she landed hard on the ground. *Air* – she had to have *air*. She braced both hands in front of her and fought to fill her lungs. They wouldn't expand.

Black dots began swarming in front of her eyes, multiplying until they filled most of her field of vision. She could hear herself wheezing, but it sounded so far away.

Something jerked on her shoulders, and dragged her backwards about a metre. Her lungs allowed air in again, and Eve felt as if she were thawing from the inside out. She blinked rapidly, and the woods reappeared around her. She tilted her head, and saw Jess above her, pulling her across the ground.

'It's OK,' Eve gasped. 'You can stop.'

Jess let go of Eve's shoulders and dropped down on the ground next to her. 'Are you positive?' she exclaimed.

Eve nodded. 'Just let me rest a sec.' She took long, slow breaths and focused on the hot ball of power inside her until she felt completely normal – normal and *warm* – again, then she pushed herself to her feet.

'Are you sure you should be standing up already?' Jess protested. 'You looked really terrible.'

'Thanks,' Eve joked. 'But I feel fine.' Actually, now that she could concentrate on the power thrumming through her body she felt more than fine. 'It's just like yesterday. I got incredibly cold and I couldn't breathe. I don't know what would have happened if you hadn't been here to pull me back.' Except she did pretty much know. She'd have ended up one of the dead things in the woods. 'It hit me so suddenly, then it left almost as fast,' Eve continued, pushing the horrible thought away.

'It was the only thing I could think to do,' Jess answered. 'You got better when Luke pulled you back from the place before, so I tried it.'

Eve looked around. 'You know, this is almost where we were yesterday. Remember, we were practically up to where the woods end in East Hampton.'

'Let's get away from here,' Jess said. She gave Eve's arm a tug.

'We're the Deepdene Witch and a kung fu master. We don't need to run away from anything,' Eve told her. She wished she had something to direct her power at, something to *fight*.

Jess gave a sharp nod. 'You're right. But we do need to figure out what's doing this to you. To *you* specifically,' she added. 'I didn't get even a little shiver and I was standing right where you were. The guys were fine yesterday too.'

'That's true.' Eve hadn't really thought about that part. She took out her iPhone. She used the GPS app to pinpoint her position on the map. Then zoomed in closer, closer. 'We're only a few steps away from the official borderline between Deepdene and East Hampton,' she murmured.

'Ooo-kay.' Jess said slowly. 'And that matters why? It'd be weird if the official border did anything to you.'

'My life has been all about the weird since school started,' Eve reminded her, not that Jess needed a reminder. She'd seen most of the weird firsthand. 'And don't you think it's also weird that I'd have the same reaction in the same place?'

'Yeah, that's weird.' Jess peered over Eve's shoulder at the map. 'All right, we have a hypothesis. Ms Whittier would say the next step is an experiment.' Ms Whittier was one of the school biology teachers.

'With me as the lab rat,' Eve said.

Jess winced. 'Sorry.'

'I think what I need to do is try to cross the border in a different spot,' Eve said, dreading the possibility of feeling another blast of freezing pain and being unable to breathe. 'Let's walk down that way, then I'll give it a shot.'

'Maybe you can use this for the science fair next year. You know your mom would pass out with joy if you entered,' Jess joked as they began walking, but Eve could hear the worry in her friend's voice.

'You're not going to believe this, but it's been a whole two days since she last talked to me about the state of my extra-curricular activities and how important they are to getting into the right school. Two days. As in two!'

'Wouldn't it be great if you could use being the saviour of our town as an extra-curricular? Now *that* would be impressive,' Jess commented.

'*That* would get me a long stay in a psychiatric hospital,' Eve countered.

'Good point. Guess you'll have to join the choir or something,' Jess said.

They walked for about a quarter of a mile. Eve checked the map. 'Let's try here. The border curves out up ahead.' She turned to face the invisible boundary and sucked in a deep, deep breath, as though that might help if her lungs iced up again. Then she started towards it.

'Oh, Eve, ick! Dead-thing alert,' Jess called.

Eve stopped in her tracks. 'I see it.' She wished she hadn't. It was a small possum, and its throat was cut, just like the squirrels and Pumpkin the cat. Its fur was splotched with blood. 'Poor th—' She didn't finish. It was starting. The tingling in her arms told her that the goose bumps had popped up, and a moment later her teeth began to chatter.

'Stop there,' Jess said. 'You don't need to keel over. The same thing is happening, right?'

Eve took three big steps back, and it began to feel like May again. 'Yeah, it was happening.' She rubbed her arms with her hands, even though the goose bumps had disappeared. The East Hampton side of the border didn't look any different from the Deepdene side. What was going on? Why did this keep happening to her – and just to her?

'When's the last time you left town?' Jess asked.

Eve thought back. 'It was before the quarantine when Amunnic was here.'

A nasty plague came to any place where Amunnic was. It was actually a good thing – a kind of advance warning system, which also stopped the demon drinking your blood if you caught it. The Center for Disease Control didn't know that though, and so Deepdene had been put into quarantine. 'I think it was the week before that we went to your cousin's party in Montauk.'

'Oh, yeah. Right,' Jess said. 'So something has happened between that day and yesterday; something that won't let you out of town.'

'Something powerful,' Eve said.

Jess's brow furrowed. 'Do you think we've got another demon on the loose?'

Chapter Five

'I think it's time to give the third musketeer a call,' Eve said as she and Jess started home. 'Luke's going to want to know what happened.'

'Do we have to be musketeers? I'd rather be Charlie's Angels,' Jess said.

'Fine by me. As long as you're the one who tells Luke he's a kickass girl.' Eve pulled out her cell, and a second later Luke was saying 'hello' into her ear. She hadn't realized exactly how much she'd wanted to hear his voice.

'Hey, Boo-Boo.' Eve decided it was time to find the perfect he's-my-boyfriend nickname for Luke. 'I had another one of those episodes in the woods,' she told him.

'What? Are you OK?' he cried. 'And did you just call me Boo-Boo?'

Cross Boo-Boo off the list. He'd sounded almost

as horrified by the nickname as he had by what happened in the woods. 'I'm fine. Jess pulled me back, Pork Chop,' Eve added as an experiment.

'Pork Chop? Uh, could I talk to Jess for a minute?'

'Luke's afraid I got some brain damage out there,' Eve told Jess. 'I'm trying to find a nickname for you, that's all,' she explained to Luke. 'I'm guessing you don't like Pork Chop either.'

Luke laughed. 'You can call me anything you want as long as you're all right.'

'I am. I swear. And the two of us figured something out. When the cold feeling hits me, I'm right at the town boundary between Deepdene and East Hampton. Freaky, right?'

'Big yeah,' Luke said. 'I'm just over at the Y, playing some b-ball. We're almost done. Want to meet me at my place? We should try to figure this out.'

'Luke wants us to come over,' Eve told Jess.

'We'll be there,' she said to Luke as Jess nodded hard. 'Bye, Love Boodle.' She hung up before she could get Luke's response to that one. She and Jess began walking faster. Eve figured Jess was almost as eager as she was to get out of the woods and over to Luke's. If this was another demon attack, they'd figure out together what they had to do. They always did.

'If there's badness, I hope pretty soon we'll have something I can kick,' Jess said. She slammed one leg straight out to the side in a kung fu move. She was getting good.

'And I hope pretty soon I have something I can zap,' Eve agreed as they reached the edge of the woods. She had all kinds of power. She could feel it now, coiled inside her, and she wanted to use it. She *needed* to use it.

'I just want to run into the D&G boutique on the way,' Jess said. 'They're only holding the dress for me until the end of the day, and I don't want to let it go.'

'You're getting it?' Eve asked. They stepped out of the woods and turned onto Main Street.

'I know there are hundreds of other dresses out there, and we haven't even been to New York, but . . .' Jess gave a little shrug.

'It looks awesome on you,' Eve said, because it did, and because she wanted to be a good friend. She didn't add that it would also look awesome on her. Or that she'd had dibbies on it.

'We still have to make our trip to the city, though,' Jess said. 'I need shoes, and a clutch—'

'And frozen hot chocolate,' Eve added.

'And that, absolutely,' Jess said.

'It won't work very well if I can't cross the town line, though,' Eve said, frowning, as they made their way down Main Street.

'We'll get you out, even if we have to dig a tunnel,' Jess promised.

Eve knew she'd do it too. 'I'll wait for you out here,' she said when they reached the boutique. 'I'm just loving being in the sunshine. When I get hit with that – whatever it is – it's like I've walked into a blizzard.'

'Are you still cold?' Jess asked.

Eve shook her head. 'It goes away really fast. But the sun still feels good.' She tilted her face up, letting the rays stroke her skin.

'Be right back.' Jess headed into the shop and was back out a few minutes later with a big bag and a big smile. 'Now on to Luke's. Or do I get to call him Love Boodle too?'

'You can try,' Eve told her. 'But I'm not going to be responsible for what happens if you do. I don't think it's going to make the cut for his pet name.'

'My vote – Hugalumps,' Jess offered.

The rectory was only a few blocks from the boutique. They came up with – and discarded – Luke boyfriend names all the way there. When they arrived, Luke was out front, waiting for them. He hurried over to Eve and wrapped her in his arms. 'You're sure you're OK?' he asked.

'Absolutely. And I'll be more than OK once we figure out what's going on,' Eve said.

'Come on in, and we'll get at it,' Luke said. 'But later, I'm taking you out and we're going to have fun, with no talking or even thinking about demons.'

'Does that invitation include me, Numnums?' Jess used the silliest name she and Eve had been able to come up with.

'If you bring Seth,' Luke answered. 'I'm not sure I can handle a date with the two of you.'

'You definitely can't. Together, we're way too much woman for you,' Eve told him as he ushered them inside. He got them settled at the kitchen table with sodas and jalapeño kettle chips.

'I was thinking maybe the first thing we should do is call the Order,' Luke said, his voice losing all its teasing tone. Time to get down to business.

'We could do some research online first,' Eve suggested. 'See if there's anything about – I don't know – paranormal phenomena along borderlines.' The Order had a lot of information in their archives. She realized that. But . . . they knew she was part demon now that they'd tested her blood. Their attitude towards her was different: they were wary of her, maybe even a little suspicious. She didn't want to go running to them every time something strange happened in Deepdene, not when she felt as if they didn't trust her.

'It couldn't hurt to check with them, though,' Jess said. 'We can do our own research while they search through their archives.' She and Luke both looked at Eve, waiting for her response.

'Sure, let's call them,' she finally said. 'You talk, Luke, OK?'

'Yeah.' He grabbed the phone. 'I'll put it on speaker.' Luke pulled a business card out of his wallet, the card that Callum had given him. Eve hoped that Callum was available. She didn't want to have to deal with Alanna, the only other Order member they'd met since Payne.

Alanna hadn't liked Eve even before she found out that Eve was part demon. She'd seemed jealous that Eve had inherited demon-killing power, while Alanna could only fight demons with one of the Order's magical swords. Also, Alanna always flirted with Luke. Always. She obviously wasn't serious about it because she was way too old for him, in her early twenties. She just did it to annoy Eve, which it did. Probably at least partly because she was ridiculously beautiful!

It was Callum who answered, so that was something. 'Luke, how are you? How are things in Deepdene?' he asked.

Hearing his voice, Eve pictured the lines carved in his face and his kind grey eyes. Then she remembered that the last time she'd seen him, those eyes had been filled with revulsion and pity.

'Hey, Callum,' Luke replied. 'Things are weird in Deepdene, which I guess means things are pretty normal. Eve and Jess are here with me, and we wanted to see if you knew of anything that could make Eve feel cold, so freezing she can hardly breathe. It's happened to her a few times out in the woods, always right at the border between our town and East Hampton.'

'Actually, I do,' Callum responded. 'At least I believe I do.'

'What is it?' Eve sounded more impatient than she'd meant to.

'Approximately a week ago, the Order spotted some indicators that Deepdene might be the target of another demon attack,' Callum said.

'Wait. A *week* ago? Why didn't you tell us?' Luke

demanded. 'What kind of demon attack are we talking about?'

'We came up with our own way to keep you three and the town safe,' Callum said, not responding to Luke's request for information on the possible attack. 'We were able to put a . . . let's call it a protective field around Deepdene that no demon can cross. We didn't know that it would affect Eve. Honestly, a human who has some demon blood isn't something we've had much experience with.'

'So it's not letting me cross, since I'm part demon.' Eve felt her face go hot with anger. 'Your protective field trapped me here.' Her voice rose with each word. 'And you didn't even bother to say anything about any of it! It's my duty to protect everyone in this town, and you didn't think I needed to know we might be attacked?'

Jess put her hand on Eve's arm. Eve knew her friend was trying to calm her down. But what the Order had done was horrific. They'd put everyone Eve loved, everyone in her whole town, in peril, just because they'd decided they could do a better job protecting Deepdene than she could. 'How could you possibly think you had any right to do this?' she rushed on.

'As I said, we were very concerned about the possibility of a demon attack,' Callum said.

Hearing him say the word 'demon', and imagining that revulsion in his eyes, a new idea slammed into Eve. She grabbed the phone. She knew Callum could hear her since she was on speaker, but actually holding the phone made her feel like she was getting right in his face, and that's what she wanted.

'I don't believe there were any indicators,' Eve cried. The heat in her face had spread to her whole body. She was surprised her skin wasn't lobster red. 'I don't believe anyone at the Order thought there was going to be a demon attack. And I don't believe you didn't know the barrier would affect me. You put that field up for *me*. Like a prison! Because I'm a demon, right? Who knows what I'm going to do some day? I might snap and go on a cross-country killing spree.'

'Evie, nobody thinks that,' Jess gasped.

'The Order knows that you've taken on every demon that's come here – and won,' Luke said at almost the same time, so his words overlapped with Jess's. 'You and the Order are on the same side.'

'You think that. But Callum doesn't. The Order made a cage for me!' Eve's hair began to whip around her face as if a wind had started up inside the house. It crackled with electricity.

'You're getting too upset, Eve. Relax, OK?' Luke said.

'I have every confidence—' Callum began.

Eve refused to listen to him. 'Now that you know I'm part demon, you think I can't be trusted!'

But there was no answer. Because the phone had melted in Eve's hand.

Eve ran blindly down the street. All she wanted was to get away – away from everyone. Callum was treating her like she was evil, Luke was all just 'Relax' and Jess was acting like Callum hadn't said what he'd actually said. Neither of them had her back. Her feet threw up sparks when they hit the sidewalk, and she could feel her fingers prickling. They had to be sparking too.

Get out of sight, she ordered herself. She was heading towards the most populated part of Main Street, the blocks where all the boutiques and restaurants were. Someone would see her there. Lots of someones. Then she'd get locked away. Everyone would be terrified of her. Her family, her friends, everyone. Even Luke and Jess would be freaked if they could see her so out of control. Wait. They had. They'd seen her kill the phone.

God, they were probably making arrangements with Callum right now to round her up and stop her from destroying Deepdene.

Through her panic, Eve registered the treetops of the woods. That's where she had to go. She'd stay away from the border. And if there was a demon lurking there – well, good. She had juice to spare.

She cut across the lawn of the closest house, tore through the side gate, ran across the backyard, then scrambled over the fence, splinters driving into her palm. She heard a ripping sound. At least she was wearing her distressed jeans. Hopefully they'd just be a little more fashionably torn.

And she was out of sight, in the woods, still running. The grass withered under her feet. The leaves on one of the maples flared with blue fire, then turned black and crumbled to ash. Eve struggled to pull the power back into her body, but she'd lost control of it. Maybe Callum and the Order were right. Maybe the world did need to be protected from her. 'Back,' she ordered her power. 'Get back.'

But just the thought of the Order and their Eve-proof force field made the heat within her surge even higher. It was going to consume the woods like a wildfire. It was going to consume *her*.

Suddenly Eve knew exactly what to do with her out-of-control power. It wanted out? Fine. She knew exactly where to send it. She slowed down to a trot. This time she needed to stop the moment she first felt cold. There was no one to pull her back. If she wasn't careful she could end up suffocating.

The grass continued to die as she jogged deeper into the woods, and the smell of burning leaves and branches filled her nose. At least the flames flared and died. She wasn't really starting a forest fire. No worries there, Smokey Bear.

Eve thought it was getting the tiniest bit harder to move forward. She brought her pace down to a walk, and held her arms out in front of her, ignoring the sparks zinging from her fingers. The moment she saw goose bumps, she stopped.

Usually, she'd concentrate on her power until she felt it gather into a hot ball in her chest. But it didn't need to gather now. It was already flowing. She just needed to aim it. Eve thrust out her hands with a cry that felt like it came up all the way from her stomach. Lightning bolts, silver with molten red tips, sizzled as they shot from her fingers.

Eve kept up the attack on the spot where she knew the force field was present. Her rage seemed to give her power an extra boost. She sent it all, everything that was in her, until only a tiny spark remained. Then she cautiously moved forward, slowly, slowly. The air moved easily in and out of her lungs. Her skin remained warm.

I did it! she thought after she'd taken a few more steps. *The barrier is down. No more cage for Eve. They never should have thought they could keep me contained. They have no idea how powerful I am.* She threw her arms up in triumph.

'Eve!'

'Eve!'

Startled, Eve dropped her arms and spun round.

Luke and Jess had followed her. Eve gestured around her. 'That protective field no demon can cross? I just blasted it away.' She grinned. She felt awesome! More powerful than she ever had. She'd found a way to use her roiling power without hurting anyone – and, bonus, she'd smashed the barrier!

Her friends stared at her, wide-eyed.

Luke shoved his blond hair off his forehead. 'Are you sure that was a good idea?'

'Yes,' Eve said.

Luke frowned. 'I'm not convinced that you're right about the Order, Eve. There's a good possibility that they put up the field to protect us. We have no reason to think Callum was lying about a demon coming to town. Maybe you should have waited—'

'So I should just be happy to never leave Deepdene again in my whole life?' Eve demanded, interrupting him. 'Because I happen to have inherited something the Order doesn't approve of? Are you even thinking about what that means? People would find out about me. What am I supposed to tell my parents when they want us to take a family vacation, or go into the city to see a play? What about school trips to the museums or to Washington, DC? If I can't leave without dying, don't you think that will make people a little suspicious?'

'But running through town with fire shooting from your fingers won't?' Luke burst out, voice filled with frustration.

Eve felt as though he'd slapped her. How could Luke think even for a second that this protective field was right? He couldn't if he really cared about her. 'The Order was formed to fight demons,' she said, her voice shaking. 'That's all they see when they see me – a demon. That's why they did this.'

'Maybe,' Luke said.

'I can't believe you don't trust me.' She felt completely betrayed.

'Eve, that's not what I said. I don't know what the truth is. All I'm saying is, I don't think you do, either. We need more information.'

She turned to Jess. 'You believe me, don't you?' Jess hesitated. Eve shook her head. 'Thanks. You're supposed to be my best friend, so just . . . thanks a lot.' That barrier had almost killed her. Luke and Jess had both witnessed that. And they still weren't sure what the Order did was wrong.

'You didn't let me answer,' Jess protested. 'What I was going to say was, we need to focus on what's important. If there is going to be a demon attack on Deepdene – and I agree that there's a possibility the Order was lying about that – but if there is even a chance there's going to be attack, then the three of us need to be preparing. Doing our research. Doing what we do. We shouldn't be fighting with each other.'

But if they weren't against the barrier, they were against her. Didn't they understand that? They had to choose sides, and they were choosing to side against her.

'I can protect the town from anything that happens, especially now that I can absorb outside energy. I'll go to the power plant, juice up, and that's all the preparation necessary,' Eve said hotly. 'I don't need your help. I don't want any help from people who don't believe in me.'

She strode past them, back towards town. 'Eve, wait!' Jess cried. Eve didn't slow down, but she heard Jess running after her.

Luke didn't call her back. He didn't follow her.

And that was fine by Eve.

What was that? Luke stared after Eve, trying to figure out how things had gone nuclear so fast. All he'd been trying to say was that there was a possibility the Order was right about the potential demon attack and that they should've left the protective barrier up, just until they knew for sure. He wasn't trying to defend their decision not to tell Eve – or any of them – what they'd done. Luke didn't think there was any good defence for that. If they'd had any inkling that their force field might affect her, they should have told her about it. They could have gotten her killed!

He turned and stared back down the black path Eve had created with her powers. He'd never seen them so wild before. On either side of the scorched grass, trees had big leafless patches and singed branches and trunks. It gave him the creeps.

Eve had let herself lose control. At least she'd gotten

herself away from people before she blew. If she hadn't . . . His stomach seized up. This couldn't happen again, no matter how angry she got. She had to understand that.

Impulsively, he turned away from the path and began to walk aimlessly through the woods. It wouldn't do any good to catch up to Eve until he had a strategy of some kind. Plus, Jess was with her. Maybe Eve would listen to Jess.

Crap. Was that another dead animal? He veered towards the dark lump he'd spotted. Yeah, it was a raccoon. Throat slit, just like the rest. He scanned the area, looking for more. He didn't see any, but he realized that he was pretty much in line with the spot where Eve had smashed through the Order's invisible barrier.

There had been a dead squirrel near where she'd hit the force field the day before. Something started itching in his brain, something he felt like he should remember. It took him a minute, then it came to him. Jess's dad had said that a friend of his saw a dog lying on the road outside of town, a dog that had been killed.

He wondered exactly how far outside town the dog had been. Could it have been on the border between

Deepdene and East Hampton? That would make four murdered animals along the line of the force field. And there were supposed to be some other animals that had gone missing in Deepdene. Where were they? Luke walked up to the raccoon, then turned and walked in a straight line towards the place where Eve had stood, on the alert for more of the tortured animals. He noticed that there was a thin dark line on the ground, running right by where he was searching. He knelt down and ran his finger along a short section of it. When he looked at his finger, it was stained a dark rust colour. *Stained with blood,* he thought.

He straightened up and kept walking, following the line of dried blood. He passed the spot where Eve had stood, and about four metres after that, he found a blue jay. Dead. Its neck slit, sliced clean through.

Luke's heart began to thud almost painfully as he continued forward, following the unbroken line of blood, his eyes locked on the ground. Something white snagged his gaze and when he hurried up to it, he found a cat. Throat cut. It was like some strange, unholy ritual had been performed along the border of Deepdene, ringing the town with blood and death.

OK, so the force field wasn't the work of a demon.

The Order had been behind that, and it apparently worked *against* demons. But these animals had been placed exactly where the force field had been, which seemed too much of a coincidence. Who – or what – had done this horrible ritual? And what was it for?

Chapter Six

Jess chased down Main Street after Eve. She'd catch her, no problem. Jess was way faster than Eve, powers or no powers.

What's the plan when you do catch her? a little voice in the back of Jess's head asked. Jess slowed down the tiniest bit in response. What *was* she going to do? Yeah, she was faster, yeah, she was a kung-fu prodigy, but Eve could turn her into ash, just the way she had the grass and trees back in the woods.

Can, but won't. It's Eve. It's Eve, Jess told herself. She shoved aside her fears and began to full-out sprint. She reached Eve's side about fifteen seconds later.

'Stop,' Jess ordered, stepping in front of her. 'Just stop and talk to me, OK?'

Eve did stop. But she planted her hands on her hips and gave Jess a hard stare. 'Why? I already know what you think. You and Luke. You think I need to be contained because I'm a – a what I am,' she finished, as if suddenly aware of the people strolling up and down the sidewalk.

'Neither of us said that,' Jess protested. 'Neither of us said anything like that. Be fair.'

Eve snorted. 'Fair? Was that barrier fair? It almost killed me!'

'And that's horrible. So horrible, we need to come up with a new word for something that is even more than horrible,' Jess answered. 'But *I* didn't put up the barrier, Evie.'

The use of her friend's nickname seemed to calm her down a little. 'I know you didn't. But you act like it's not evil. And it is. What the Order did to me was evil.'

This wasn't the time to make the argument that the Order might have been trying to protect the town, trying to stop something evil from coming in.

'Look, we can't have an actual conversation about this standing on the street. You know you're going to forgive me, because you know that I'd never take sides against you, even if it felt like I did,' Jess rushed on. She didn't want Eve to start arguing. 'Here's what we're going to do. We're going to my house, where I'm going to make you some hot chocolate. We're both going to calm down a little. Then we'll figure out what we should be doing. Because there might be a demon ready to attack. And there's the barrier that can kill you. We have a lot more important things to be doing than fighting with each other,' Jess told Eve.

Which is why Jess wasn't going to bring up the way Eve had basically accused her of not being Eve's friend. It hurt, and it was completely unfair – Jess had proved again and again that she was always going to be there for Eve – but she was going to let it go. It wasn't the time to fight. That hadn't just been something she'd said to calm Eve down.

Eve sighed. Then she nodded.

Jess looped her arm through Eve's, and they began walking towards Jess's house.

Jess realized that tiny tremors were rippling through her. Seeing Eve's powers get out of control had shocked her to the core. Eve had lost her grip on them before, especially when they first started appearing. But shorting out the TV or melting a lipstick were in a whole different category to setting trees on fire. If the leaves and branches hadn't turned to ash almost immediately, Eve could have accidentally burned down the whole town.

'I'm not sure hot chocolate is going to do it,' Eve

replied. 'I'm still just so anti-calm.' She began flexing her fingers, and Jess did a check for sparks, trying to keep Eve from noticing that she was looking.

'Did I mention chocolate whipped cream? Did I mention that the chocolate whipped cream would be a double serving? Did I further mention there would be Mint Milanos?' Jess asked. She knew no amount of chocolate would be able to soothe Eve, but pretending it might made Jess feel better. Who knew? Maybe pretending would make Eve feel better too.

Eve did try to force a smile, but Jess could see tears shimmering in her deep blue eyes. She wasn't sure if they were angry tears or sad tears or both. 'Luke and I practically just got together, and now I feel like we're going to have to break up.'

'Eve, no! You had a fight. One fight,' Jess protested.

'One fight about him not trusting me,' Eve said. 'That equals – what do you think – about ten regular fights?'

'No way. Maybe three,' Jess answered, torn between her loyalty to Eve and her deep feeling that Luke had been, well, kind of right. 'But, Evie, he didn't really say he doesn't trust you. He – and I – we just thought there was a possibility the Order could be right about a potential demon attack on Deepdene. That's all. We didn't think they were right not to tell you what was going on. Especially not after you've taken down every demon that came here.'

'*Aaarrrgh!*' Eve let out a growl. 'Let's not talk about it any more. It makes me crazy.'

'OK, topic change. Let's see . . .' Jess tried to think of something fun and light to take Eve's mind off things. The prom, maybe? But Jess couldn't shake the feeling that Eve might still be upset about the Dolce & Gabbana dress, even though Jess had a place to wear it and Eve didn't, not really. Eve had said the dress looked awesome on Jess and acted happy, but they'd been friends for a long time, and Jess could tell when Eve was faking it. And she had been, at least a little.

'Maybe we should have a Christmas in May movie festival,' Jess suggested as they turned onto her street. 'We could watch *Elf.* You have to at least giggle at *Elf.*'

'Sorry, Jess,' Eve said. 'I'm still too angry to laugh. I'm so mad at Luke! Even though, like you said, the Order could be right about an attack. They know a lot about demons, even if they are a bunch of arrogant pigs who want to trap me in Deepdene for ever.'

Jess didn't mind that Eve had said she didn't want to talk about it any more, then almost immediately started talking about it again. Sometimes a girl just needed to vent, even if she was sick of venting.

'They were probably only thinking about keeping demons out. Callum even said they weren't sure how the barrier would affect you, since you just have some demon blood,' Jess answered. There were away from Main Street now, away from the crowd, so it was safe to use the 'D' word.

'I have to try and let it go,' Eve continued. 'I shot out all my power at the barrier around town, and I can already feel the power building up again. Sometimes it's as if the Deepdene Witch energy feeds on my emotions.'

'Let's see how you feel after my hot-chocolate-chocolate-whipped-cream-Mint-Milano-*Elf* plan,' Jess said. She hoped it worked. She didn't like the idea of Eve's power getting so hot again so soon. 'If that doesn't do it, we'll—'

Jess broke off, staring at her house. She could hardly believe her eyes.

'We'll what?' Eve asked.

Jess grabbed her best friend's arm. 'Up there, by the bushes. Is that Simon?' That's the last thing she needed. She'd just gotten started on the Eve-calming.

Eve narrowed her eyes and studied Jess's house as

they approached. 'It's him all right. Sitting there reading a book on your lawn. I can't believe it. I heard you
on the phone. You made it completely clear you had
no interest in him.'

'And then he wrote me that letter,' Jess said. She
kept her eyes on Simon. He sprang up as soon as
she and Eve turned onto the walkway to her house,
dropping the huge leather-bound book he'd been
reading.

'I was w-waiting for you,' he stammered.

'This is *so* not a good time,' Jess told him. She
stopped, Eve beside her. 'If fact, it's never going to be
a good time, Simon, OK? Please leave me alone!' She
sounded a little harsher than she meant to, but it had
been a helluva long day, and that letter he'd written –
it was creepy.

Simon blinked a couple of times, then rushed past
them, stumbling in his hurry to leave.

'Your book!' Eve called. She picked it up for him
and held it out. Simon turned back and snatched it
away, two bright red patches appearing high on his
paper-white cheekbones. Then he bolted.

'OK, I admit it, I'm officially in a state of extreme
worry,' Jess said, her eyes finding a drop of dried
blood on a flagstone that her dad had missed when he

hosed off the grass and walkway. 'He was sitting almost exactly where we found Pumpkin.'

'I was about to say I can't imagine Simon doing anything like that,' Eve said slowly. 'But then I realized I don't really know him. It doesn't seem like anyone at school does. He's always alone.'

'What was that book he had? Did you see?' Jess asked.

'It just had a bunch of weird markings on the front,' Eve told her.

'I keep thinking about those strange words – if they even were words – he said to me on the phone,' Jess said. Her eyes kept darting back to the drop of dried blood. 'Do you think it could have been some kind of curse? I mean an actual curse, not a "darn it" kind of curse. Maybe that book . . . maybe it's like a spell book.'

'All I saw was the cover.' Eve frowned. 'We'll just have to keep a close eye on him.' She looped one arm around Jess's shoulders. 'Don't worry. Your best friend is the Deepdene Witch and you are nearly a superhero with your mad kung-fu skills. If we can handle Malphus and the wargs and Amunnic, we can definitely handle Simon.'

Jess nodded. It had been scary seeing Eve with her

power so out of control back in the woods, but now Jess was grateful that Eve had her special abilities – abilities she'd always used to fight evil. 'Let's go in and chocolatize ourselves.'

'Sounds good,' Eve replied. She seemed better. Maybe it was good – in a weird way – that Simon had showed up. He was quite the distraction. It seemed like maybe Eve's attention had just gotten sucked away from Luke and the Order and over to Jess's crazy stalker.

Jess opened the door. As they headed towards the kitchen through the living room, they almost walked right past Peter without noticing him. He was slumped down in one of the armchairs, staring at the TV – even though it wasn't on. Weird.

'You OK, Peter?' Jess asked her little brother.

'Peter?' Eve repeated.

Peter jumped, as if he had been dozing, then he turned towards them and smiled. 'Just having a little brain vacation. In my head, I was in Hawaii. How great was that trip last summer?'

Jess's family had gone to the islands for vacation, and, of course, she'd convinced her parents that Eve had to come with them. It wasn't hard. They loved Eve.

'So, what's the plan? If it involves food, I'm in.'

Jess smiled. It was good to have her brother back to his usual self, annoying as that usual self could often be.

YOU OK? CALL ME.

Luke sent the text to Eve, but he doubted it would get a response. He'd already left two voicemails and heard nothing. He flopped back on his bed and stared up at the ceiling. Man, she'd been pissed off at him. He'd never seen her even close to that angry before. The way her power had exploded out of her hands . . .

Her power was stronger than he'd ever imagined. He had been scared that she might hurt herself today. Or take out the entire Deepdene Woods. She'd managed to blast through a supposedly demon-proof barrier. If the Order was right about an attack, a demon could already have arrived in town through the hole she'd made.

So the question was: should he alert the Order that their protective barrier was now down? If he did, Eve would see it as another betrayal. She'd see it as him siding against her. Which he wasn't.

He'd seen Eve go head-to-head with demons. She was the opposite of dangerous to the town. She'd saved it again and again. Her power was a force for good, at least as long as she could control it.

But that wasn't the question. The question was whether or not he should tell the Order that the demon block was no longer in place. After all, their job was to fight demons too. They should know if one of their demon-fighting weapons had been compromised. But what would their attitude to Eve be once they heard she had destroyed it?

Luke checked his phone, even though he knew he wasn't going to get a message back from Eve. And, sure enough, he hadn't gotten a message back from her. He went over to his desk so he could check his email. Nothing from Eve. Because that's how furious she was at him.

He used his feet to swivel his desk chair back and forth. Tell the Order? Don't tell the Order? Possibly put Deepdene in danger? Definitely make Eve even madder at him?

If a demon did come to town, Eve could handle it without the Order. She'd done it before. Still . . .

She'd done it before, she could probably do it again, but he couldn't risk it. What if she didn't get to the demon in time? What if their first clue about where the demon was turned out to be a dead person? He couldn't deal with it if someone got hurt – or killed – because he'd sat on his butt, too afraid that his girlfriend would be angry at him.

With a sigh, Luke opened a new email window and began to write. He hit send before he had a chance to change his mind. The Order had the info now. It had been the right thing to do, even though, when he thought about Eve, it felt so wrong.

Luke decided to spend some time studying for finals. It was better than sending Eve even more texts and leaving her even more voicemails. That was just pathetic, but before he could reach for his biology book, an IM popped up on the computer. It was from Alanna.

AlannaG: So Eve took down the barrier. I don't blame her. Callum shouldn't have had it erected without knowing how it would affect her.

Huh. Luke hadn't been expecting that. Alanna didn't usually take Eve's side. He typed a response back.

Sinbad: Why didn't the Order tell us what was going on?

He used the screen name Sinbad because he was a preacher's son and knew sin was bad. Also, Sinbad, the legendary sailor, was apparently a real badass.

AlannaG: Told Callum it was a bad idea. Eve is powerful. She should be used as an asset. That means telling her if there's a problem. Not going behind her back to protect the town. She's more protection than anything we can do.

Luke wasn't crazy about the word 'asset.' It made Eve sound like a *thing* rather than a girl. Like something less than human. But he was glad Alanna realized the Order hadn't done the right thing.

Sinbad: Why did he want to keep it secret?

AlannaG: Who knows? The Order has politics just like everyplace.

Sinbad: What do you think about the dead animals we've found around the border of town? Throats slit. Did a demon kill them?

AlannaG: Possible. Definitely some dark power ritual. Dangerous.

Sinbad: Advice??

AlannaG: I'm coming to check it out. Be there tomorrow. Don't worry. We'll figure it out – you, me, Eve, Jess.

Eve wouldn't like that. She wouldn't like anyone from the Order showing up right now, but she especially wouldn't want Alanna anywhere near her. At least this time Alanna was acting like she and Eve were on the same side. And she'd actually mentioned Jess. Usually Alanna behaved as if Jess didn't even exist because she wasn't useful to the Order. Luke had the sword, obviously, which is what put him in the 'useful' category.

But even if Eve didn't like it, Luke felt better just knowing that more help was on the way.

Sinbad: Thanks. We might need the assist. See you then.

Luke knew he'd done the right thing, even if he

had gone behind Eve's back. He just hoped he could convince Eve of that.

'Feeling better?' Jess asked.

Eve nodded, lingering in the open front door of Jess's house before she headed home. 'You?'

Jess nodded. 'So are you going to take pity on the boy and answer one of his calls or texts?'

'I suppose.' Eve sighed. 'No, I definitely will. Eventually. I'm still a little angry around the edges, so I might wait at little longer. I don't want to call back just so we can get in another fight.'

'Just remember, when you make up you can have all that make-up making out,' Jess teased.

Which would be nice. Very nice. Extremely nice. If only Luke hadn't acted like such a jerk.

Slurquish.

'Did you hear that?' Eve asked, spinning round so she was facing the street.

'What?' Jess cried. 'Is Simon back?' She crowded up beside Eve, trying to get a better view.

'No, it didn't sound like a person. I don't know what it sounded like. But something not right. Something—'

Slurquish. Slurquish.

'There it is again!' Eve exclaimed. The sky had almost darkened and it was difficult to see, but Eve thought something was moving in the shadows across the street. 'I'm going to check it out,' she told Jess.

'Not by yourself. I'm coming too,' Jess answered. She sounded a little anxious and a lot determined.

They hurried across the lawn, and just as they reached the sidewalk, the streetlamps turned on with a soft click. And Eve saw it clearly. A demon. A big one. Jess let out a gasp.

The thing was massive, but huge as it was, it looked as if it had been slapped together without much care. Its torso was an ill-defined lump. Its arms and legs were thick, with no knees or elbows; its hands and feet were slabs with only a few fingers and toes.

Its head appeared half finished too. The demon had a mouth, a huge gaping hole that filled more than half its face. Its nose was only two ragged holes. If it had eyes, Eve couldn't see them.

'Wow,' Eve said. 'I have seen some ugly demons, but this one wins Best in Show.'

It turned at the sound of her voice, so maybe there were ears on that misshapen head too.

'Are *you* the big bad demon the Order was afraid of?' she asked the thing.

Jess let out a soft whistle. 'Now I'm mad at them too. They should have warned us about the smell.' She waved her hand back and forth in front of her nose. 'I bet I could kill you with a super-size can of deodorant,' she called to the demon. She didn't sound nervous any more. She must have switched into kick-ass mode.

'Let's show the Order that we don't need their help,' Eve said grimly. 'Warning or no warning, I can take this bad boy.'

Eve focused on her power, glad that her anger had already started building back up. She wouldn't want to face this thing with an empty tank. The energy coiled into a tight ball just below her sternum. Just as she was about to throw out her hands and slam her lightning into the demon, it charged towards her, its feet making that disgusting squishing sound.

It swung out one arm, and it stretched impossibly far. Eve didn't have time to fire. She began to back up, but it was too late.

'Hands off her!' Jess shouted. She gave a round-house kick that connected with a wet thunk. The demon's hand and half of its arm fell to the ground, spasming. 'That's right!' Jess cried in triumph. 'I said hands off!'

The demon let out a gurgling growl. Its already huge mouth stretched open even further, revealing double rows of teeth. 'Keep your mouth shut too!' Eve yelled. She sent lightning bolts straight into the thing's maw, and steam poured out – steam that reeked of rotten fish and was flecked with blood.

Before Eve could strike again, the demon grabbed her around the waist with its remaining hand. It pulled her against it, and she felt its squishy body ooze over her skin, sucking her inside like some kind of mud pit. Her hands were trapped in the thick slime of its torso and the stench of the demon over-whelmed her.

Eve held her breath and forced herself to think. Her hands were inside the thing's body. Could she shoot her lightning bolts that way? She didn't know. But she had to try.

Her hands tingled and her arms shook as she tried to let the power burst out of her fingertips. Was it having any effect on the creature?

Jess didn't wait to find out. She aimed a fierce side kick at the spot where the demon's knee would be – if it had a knee. The thing uttered a high wail and the bottom half of its leg fell to the ground.

It hopped sideways, frantically trying to regain its

balance, and Eve was able to yank one hand free. She zapped the demon, its flesh steaming wherever her lightning bolts hit.

'Let me do that again. It won't have a leg to stand on!' Jess cried, grinning with the excitement of the fight. She whipped round and kicked backwards at the demon's remaining leg, taking it off almost at the torso. Eve let loose another bolt of power, aimed right at the thing's head.

The demon collapsed to the ground, disintegrating until it was a puddle of goo. 'Ding, dong!' Eve said, as the foul-smelling puddle slid towards the storm drain.

'The witch is dead,' Jess finished for her. 'Except this time the witch won.'

'With the help of the soon-to-be blue belt,' Eve said. As she and Jess slapped a high-five, Eve heard footsteps. Maybe the demon hadn't been alone! She whipped towards the sound, hands already out in front of her.

'Whoa!' Luke cried. 'Just . . . whoa.'

Eve immediately let her hands fall to her sides. 'Sorry, I thought you might be something evil. We only finished killing a demon about two seconds ago.'

'That's it going down the drain,' Jess offered, nodding towards the greasy goop.

'A demon? That?' Luke raised his eyebrows, covering his nose.

'It used to be bigger. And, you know, solid,' Eve told him.

'Are you both OK?' he exclaimed. 'Sorry I didn't get here in time to help.'

'Why are you here now?' Eve asked, then realized she sounded witchy – in a bad way. 'I mean, well, you know what I mean.'

'I needed to talk to you and you wouldn't answer the phone,' Luke said simply.

'Maybe I should—' Jess took a step back towards the house, probably thinking the make-up make-out session might be starting soon.

'No, you need to hear this too, Jess,' Luke replied. He took a deep breath, as if he needed strength for whatever he was going to say. 'Eve, you're not going to like this, but I let the Order know that the force field is down. I just ... It's not that I don't trust you to protect Deepdene, but I think we need to use all the help available. At least as long as the Order doesn't keep any more secrets from us.'

Eve wiped her gooey hands on her only slightly

less gooey jeans. Luke's statement had taken a little of the happy out of her demon-killing buzz. 'Luke, there was no reason for you to do that. I told you, we don't need them. This just proves it.' She gestured to the drain and the remains of the demon. 'They were right about a demon attack coming,' she continued. 'But they were wrong about me not being able to handle it without them throwing up that barrier. I didn't need any help to get rid of Goopy.'

Jess cleared her throat loudly, while staring at Eve.

'That's wrong actually. I definitely needed Jess's help,' Eve amended quickly. 'But I always have her help against demons. And usually yours.' Yeah, she was still a little angry around the edges.

'I was trying to help when I called the Order,' Luke said defensively. 'I talked to Alanna and she agreed that they shouldn't have put up the barrier.'

'Alanna actually took Eve's side?' Jess raised an eyebrow.

'Yup. She's going to come to town tomorrow to help us figure out what's going on,' Luke said.

'Why?' Eve burst out. 'We already know what's going on.' The last person she felt like seeing right now was Alanna.

'I need to backtrack.' Luke shoved his hair away from his forehead. 'After you guys left, I realized that those dead animals we've been finding aren't random. What I mean is, they're placed all around the Deepdene town border, and there's a line of blood connecting them. That's also why I got in touch with the Order. I thought it must have been done by a demon, but I didn't know why. I figured they might have an answer.'

'I guess Goopy could have killed those poor animals,' Eve said. 'Although its hands were so squishy. It's hard to imagine it holding a knife.'

'We killed a demon!' Jess exclaimed suddenly.

'Yeah, we did.' Eve smiled at her.

'No, what I meant was, we killed a demon right in front of my house!' Jess cried. 'I was so caught up in the moment, I didn't even realize. What if Peter saw us? He's just getting back to normal.'

'Ooh,' Eve said. She hadn't thought about that either.

'I hope he didn't notice it. He was so freaked out by E— By everything,' Jess said.

By me, Eve thought sadly. *He was freaked out by me and my witch powers.*

'It's too bad the demon ended up right in front of

your house, of all places,' Luke said. Then he frowned. 'Seems kind of strange, doesn't it?'

'It was in the shadows across the street when we saw it,' Jess told him. 'Do you think it was watching my house? Or maybe it was attracted by Eve. Peter thinks she's a demon magnet.' Jess winced and glanced at Eve. 'And it does seem like demons end up coming after her.'

'It didn't seem to notice me until I said something,' Eve put in. 'I'm not sure it was expecting to find me at all.'

'Maybe,' Luke said. 'After all, Deepdene's a small town. It could just be a coincidence that the demon ended up here.'

That didn't feel right to Eve, though. Deepdene was small, yes. But there were a lot of streets. If it was a coincidence that the demon ended up on the same street as her, at the same time as her, then it was a pretty big one.

Chapter Seven

'So,' Luke said.

That was it? So?

'So,' Eve repeated. Luke was walking her home after the demon battle. She'd showered off the remains of Goopy at Jess's house and borrowed some clean clothes. She was still feeling the triumph of killing the demon. What she *wasn't* feeling was the happiness of having her boyfriend give her the apology he owed her.

'So,' he began again. 'That fight . . . I just want you to know that I do trust you. How could I not trust you? I've seen you battling demons, and you're awesome. You don't back down, no matter what.'

'Then why did you think the Order was right?' Eve asked.

'I didn't. I thought going behind your back and putting up the barrier was absolutely wrong. A hundred per cent wrong,' Luke answered. 'All I meant to say was that there was a possibility the Order had decent intel about a demon attack.'

'But, Luke, you thought I should leave the barrier. The Order made me a prisoner, and even though you say you thought it was wrong, you expected me to stay locked up!' Eve exclaimed. She had to make him understand what it had felt like to realize she'd been caged.

'I wasn't thinking of it like that. I was thinking that we needed to wait a little and get more information on what kind of attack we might be facing before you took down the force field,' Luke told her. 'But I was wrong. The Order had no right to lock you in town, not even for a few days. Not even for a few hours. You should have blasted it away, just like you did.'

He stopped and turned to face her, putting his hands on her shoulders. 'I'm so sorry, Eve. I believe in you, and I should have been right there with you, throwing rocks at the demon barrier, doing whatever I could to back you up.'

The last bit of anger Eve had been holding onto slipped away. He understood why she'd been so furious. And she understood why he'd wanted her to wait to take the barrier down. He was just trying to keep everybody safe. 'Thanks, Luke. And I'm sorry too. I should have taken more time to explain instead of just exploding. What the Order did – it made me crazy.'

They continued walking, but hand in hand now. 'I should have talked to you before I told them you'd blasted it down. The thing was – you weren't answering the phone.'

'Oh, so it's my fault,' Eve teased, relieved their first fight was over.

'Well, I'd say yeah, but I'm not ready to have another fight with you any time this century,' Luke replied.

'You don't think they're going to put it back up, do you?' she asked.

'Not without telling you,' he said. 'And, if they do, Jess and I will go attack them with swords and kung fu.'

Eve shook her head, feeling another burst of anger at Callum and the Order. 'That protective barrier completely didn't work, anyway,' she said. 'All the Order managed to do was trap that humongous goo demon in town. Think about it. Those dead animals in the woods – they were killed by the demon while the barrier was up. The demon Callum thought he was protecting Deepdene from was already inside.'

'I guess predicting demon behaviour isn't an exact science,' Luke replied.

'Which is why the Order should stop acting like it knows everything,' Eve said.

'I ought to get in touch with Alanna, tell her not to bother coming now that we – meaning you and Jess – killed the demon the Order was worried about,' Luke said. 'Although I guess she might still want to check things out.'

'Oh, let her come if she wants to,' Eve commented. Luke had said that Alanna had been on her side about the Order putting up that barrier. Maybe she wasn't all bad. And it felt right to compromise, to show Luke that she wasn't a my-way-or-the-highway girl.

They reached Eve's house, but Luke didn't let go of her hand. 'We're good, right?'

'Well, there's still one more thing,' Eve said, trying not to smile.

'Uh-oh. What else have I done?' Luke asked.

'Jess said that after our fight we had to have wild make-up making out,' Eve told him. Actually, Jess hadn't said wild. Eve had added that part.

'She did?' Luke released her hand and pulled her close to him.

'That's what she said,' Eve answered. 'Pooh Bear,' she added.

He laughed. 'Well, if we have to, we have to, Bunny. Um, Bunny something. I need a word that rhymes with Bunny.'

'You don't need anything,' Eve told him, looping her arms around his neck.

Luke lowered his lips to hers. The kiss was long, and sweet, and hot. And, yes, a little wild! 'I was wrong about not wanting to have another fight for a hundred years,' he said when he lifted his head. 'I think we should fight as much as possible, just so we can do more of this.'

He kissed her again.

'What did you get for question eight in that quiz?' Ben Flood called to Eve after school. She and Luke were heading outside to find Jess so they could all go and meet up with Alanna together.

'One over three x plus one.' She and Luke paused so she could answer. 'That was the hardest one, I thought. Glad I managed to get in some studying time last night.' She'd taken her algebra book into the bath-tub with her before going to bed. She'd showered after the Goopy fight, but she'd felt the need for a long, long bubble bath too.

'We didn't even have homework last night,' Ben said. He looked at Luke. 'You're clearly not keeping your girlfriend entertained enough if she has to study for classes where we don't even have assignments.'

Luke smiled at Eve. 'I do my best. That's all I can tell you.'

Eve flushed, thinking of all the kissing they'd done the night before. 'I studied because I knew we were going to have a quiz,' she told Ben. 'He almost always gives quizzes when they are re-running *Desperate Housewives*. Don't ask me to explain it.'

'Guess I'll have to start studying the *TV Guide*,' Ben said. 'Thanks for the tip. See you tomorrow.' He headed into the gym's side entrance.

'Got any tips for me?' Luke joked as they walked outside.

'You heard Ben. You have to work a little harder to keep your girlfriend from becoming a complete study drudge,' she answered.

He grabbed her, twisted her into a deep dip, and kissed her, getting them a round of applause from everyone in the quad.

'Nice,' Eve said, blushing as she straightened up. 'Oh, there's Jess.' She pointed across the Deepdene High parking lot. A group of kids – all seniors except for Jess – were gathered around Seth's Escalade – the Cadillac SUV was Seth's pride and joy – enjoying the afternoon sunshine and the fact that classes were over for the day.

When they walked over, they found the group in the middle of a debate about who should be eligible to be prom queen. 'What I'm saying is that if a senior guy takes a freshman girl, she should be able to be queen if he's king,' Seth said.

Eve smiled. Seth was making it sound all theoretical, but it was clear he was talking about him and Jess.

'That's not how it works,' Lindsey Vissering, captain of the cheerleading squad and a senior, told Seth. 'Forget the freshman-senior part of it for a minute. The prom queen is not the date of the prom king. The—'

'Hold up. My sister was prom queen and the guy she went with was prom king,' Dave Perry protested. 'If you don't believe me, just come to our house. There are about a million pictures of them with their crowns on.'

'But that wasn't because they were a couple,' Lindsey explained. 'Prom queen and king are voted on separately. So a couple might end up queen and king, but not because they're a couple, because they both happened to get the most votes.'

'Well, why doesn't anyone who's there get the chance to win?' Seth challenged.

'Because it's the *Senior* Prom. *Senior*,' Carrie Carrothers, also a senior – a senior who happened to be a likely pick for prom queen – told him.

'Then if I'm elected prom king, I have to do that spotlight dance, or whatever it's called, with—' Seth began.

'Who cares about the spotlight dance?' Dave interrupted. 'Who cares about the dance period? I'm all about the after party. Some of the guys were talking about that clearing in the woods instead of the beach because it's more private. But my parents are all freaked about the arsonist. You guys heard about the fire, right?'

Eve's heart fluttered. The arsonist, that was her – burning the woods on her anger-filled rampage.

'In science, Ms Whittier was saying maybe it wasn't arson. We had that weird heat wave, and she said that could have set up the conditions for a spontaneous wildfire,' Carrie told the group.

Eve stopped listening to the conversation. The back of her neck was prickling and she had the overwhelming sensation that someone was watching her. She looked over her shoulder. At first she didn't see anyone looking her way, then she spotted Simon. He was crouched down behind a car over at the edge of the lot.

Only he wasn't staring at her. He was staring at Jess, who had her arm around Seth's waist, laughing at something he'd just said. Eve shivered. Simon seemed to get more obsessed with Jess every day. *That slimy demon killed the animals in the woods*, she reminded herself. *It must have killed Pumpkin too. Pumpkin was killed in exactly the same way. Simon's obsessed, but not animal-murdering crazy.*

Even so, Eve promised herself to keep an extra close watch on Jess. Nothing bad was going to happen to the best friend of the Deepdene Witch!

Luke glanced at his watch. 'We should get going.'

Eve nodded. Alanna was meeting them at Ola's Ice Cream Shop in about ten minutes. She signalled to Jess, who gave Seth a quick kiss, then headed over to Eve and Luke.

'I told Seth I needed to study for finals with you two. Just in case it comes up,' Jess said as they started for Ola's.

'At least there's no final in history. Only that report.' Eve stopped walking, horrified.

'What?' Luke asked, looking around as if a demon might come popping out from under a car.

'I forgot to give the report in. And you know how Mr Zhang is about getting things in on time,' Eve said. 'I have to run back and get it to him before he leaves. You two go ahead. I'll be right behind you.'

'I'll order for you,' Luke called after her. 'I know what you like.'

'Aww, what a good boyfriend,' Eve heard Jess say to Luke.

Luke was her boyfriend! Sometimes that was still a little hard to believe. But they'd had their first fight and their first make-up. That made them a real couple.

It was hard to miss Alanna. Luke was willing to bet that every guy who walked into Ola's noticed her right off. It's not that she was prettier than Eve, definitely not. But there was something about her. It was as if Alanna expected to be looked at, so you looked. Today she had her long hair swept up on top of her head. With her hair up – and her shirt conveniently cut to fall off one shoulder – it was really easy to see her tattoo of roses and thorns.

Jess elbowed him. 'I'm here, which pretty much means Eve's here, so I don't think you should be staring at Alanna like that. Because if Eve was here, you wouldn't be.'

'I wasn't staring,' Luke protested. 'I was just noticing that she was here. As in, "We're meeting Alanna – and, oh, look, there she is".' He started towards the booth in the back where Alanna was sitting.

'Don't notice so hard,' Jess muttered, following close behind him.

Alanna hadn't seen them yet. She was tapping her teaspoon against the table top, frowning a little. Luke wondered what she was thinking about. The demon attack that the Order had predicted, probably. She'd be relieved to hear that Eve had already taken the demon down. Eve *and* Jess, he reminded himself. He wanted to make sure Alanna knew that Jess had held her own.

'Hey, Alanna,' Luke called as they approached. The frown disappeared, and Alanna gave them a big smile. Well, maybe it was directed a little more at him than Jess.

'It's great to see you. Sit down, sit down!' Alanna urged. 'I ordered us one of those massive sundaes they have here. It's enough for about eight people, but I couldn't resist.'

Jess sat down next to Alanna. Luke knew that she was making sure Eve would be next to Luke. Which was fine by him. No place he'd rather be.

'Where's Eve?' Alanna asked. She brushed her fingers lightly across one of the roses of her tattoo.

'She'll be right here,' Jess said quickly, before Luke could answer. 'She just needed to run back to school for a minute.'

'Well, you two fill me in on what's been happening,' Alanna said. 'I can't wait. So, you realized the barrier had been put up, and then what?'

'Like I told you, Eve used her power to take it down,' Luke replied. 'She was really upset that the Order had trapped her in town.'

'The barrier almost killed her!' Jess jumped in, eyes bright with anger on behalf of her friend. 'They really should have told her about it.'

Alanna held up both hands in mock surrender. 'I agree. I told Callum that. But, basically, I'm powerless at the Order. I'm still just a trainee,' she told them. 'So, go on. Eve took down the barrier, and then you found the dead animals all around the town border, right, Luke?'

'Yeah, and while he was doing that, Eve and I killed the demon,' Jess put in, a triumphant gleam in her eye.

Alanna's brow wrinkled. 'What? What demon?'

'A gigantic smelly one made of slime, or mud, or something,' Jess told her. 'Huge mouth, lots of teeth?'

'Is that the one the Order has in the database?' Luke asked.

Alanna shrugged. 'It doesn't ring a bell. I can look it up once I get back to the Order.' She narrowed her eyes and studied Jess. 'You killed it?'

'I took out its limbs with kung fu, and Eve zapped it into a puddle of goo,' Jess said. 'No thanks to you guys and your invisible fence around the town.'

'Yeah. In fact, since I found the dead animals inside the boundary, it means the Order put up the force field *after* the demon had already showed up in Deepdene. I want Callum to know that. He ended up putting us all in more danger, not less,' Luke said.

'OK. I'll tell him that as soon as I get back,' Alanna promised. 'Are the animals still in place? I'd like to look at them. It might give me an idea what kind of ritual was being performed.'

'I'll pass. I got a close enough look at the icky

squishiness of the animals when I got some on my shoe,' Jess said.

'I left the animals right where they were,' Luke said as the waitress delivered their mountain of ice cream. He wondered if he should still order Eve some coconut chocolate chip. That was her favourite, and he'd told her that he would order for her, but they already had enough ice cream to choke a couple of elephants. 'Is there coconut chocolate chip in this?' he called after the waitress.

'There's everything in that,' she called back. 'Every flavour, every syrup, every topping.'

That should have Eve covered, Luke decided.

'It doesn't really matter what the ritual was, does it?' Jess asked. 'The demon is dead. Eve handled it, no problem.'

'I think we should get as much info as we can on every demon that's appeared in Deepdene,' Luke said. 'And it wasn't just Eve who took care of the latest demon,' he added to Alanna. 'Jess did her share. Turns out she's some kind of martial arts phenomenon.'

'I am moving up pretty quickly in my kung-fu classes,' Jess said, smiling. Luke smiled too. It was cool how Jess had decided she was going to go out and get herself some demon-fighting moves.

'How long have you been taking lessons?' Alanna asked Jess.

'Not long, but I'm going to be testing for my blue belt soon,' Jess replied. 'Maybe my cheerleading helped me. There's a lot of kicking in cheerleading.'

'It would take quite a kick to damage a demon.' Alanna licked a little whipped cream off her upper lip.

That's true, Luke thought. *A kick probably wouldn't have made* Amunnic *even blink.* He believed that Jess's kung fu had helped kill this last demon. But it wouldn't have been as useful against the first one they'd met, Malphus. And if you tried to kick a warg, you'd probably end up without a foot.

'This demon was weird,' Jess said thoughtfully. 'I mean, I guess all demons are weird, but this one was weird because it was really squishy. Like it was only partly formed or something. Do demons ever come out half-baked?'

Alanna shook her head. 'Not really. But the varieties of demon are almost infinite. The Order keeps cataloguing them, but it's virtually impossible to keep up.'

'I'm trying to get a database of our own going,' Luke said. 'I have everything we've figured out about the portal in Deepdene, and the demons we've fought so far, and Eve's powers.'

'So where were you and your trusty sword when Eve and Jess were doing battle?' Alanna teased. 'Inputting data?'

'He wasn't needed,' Jess said playfully.

'True. I wasn't. But I still wish I'd been there,' Luke said. 'If there's a fight, I want to be there. Even if the girls don't need me to do much more than cheer them on.' Actually, he'd rather take on the demons alone. He hated Eve or Jess being in danger. But there was nothing he could do about it, at least as far as Eve was concerned. She had the power. He didn't.

For a moment Luke flashed on the damage Eve had done to the woods with that power. He hoped he never saw her lose it like that again.

'Do you practise with the sword?' Alanna asked. 'Just so you'll be ready?'

'I should, I guess,' Luke answered. 'I haven't, though.' He made a mental note to come up with a workout that used the sword. He could be a lot better with it than he was.

'Hmmm. I do a whole series of exercises with mine every morning. I'll have to share them with you.' Alanna leaned across the table and put her hand on Luke's. 'Tell me more about this database of yours.'

Luke couldn't help but notice that Jess's bright

smile immediately turned into a frown at the sight of Alanna touching him. But what was he supposed to do? Jerk his hand away? Wouldn't that be rude? He decided to leave it for a minute then pick up his spoon, which would move his hand out from under Alanna's without him making a thing of it. And it *wasn't* a thing, anyhow. It wasn't like Alanna meant anything by it. She was in her twenties and he was a freshman in high school. Alanna was just one of those touchy kinds of girls.

'What kind of data have you recorded on Eve?' she continued. 'No one in the Order has abilities like the Deepdene witches.'

'Eve's power is mind-blowing,' Luke began. 'Besides the demon-fighting, she can also read demon runes and understand demon language. Eve has—'

Jess interrupted him with some loud throat-clearing. He glanced up at her, and saw that she was looking at something over his shoulder. He followed her gaze and saw Eve standing behind him.

She did not look happy.

Chapter Eight

Eve nibbled on her bottom lip. *There's my boyfriend, holding hands with the ridiculously hot Alanna. And I'm pretty sure he was just saying something about me to her, behind my back. And he hasn't even ordered my ice cream!*

She forced herself to smile. The last thing she wanted to do in front of Alanna was look insecure and jealous. Especially because she had nothing to feel insecure and jealous about. It made total sense that they were talking about her. She was the Deepdene Witch. She'd just taken down the Order's barrier and killed a demon.

Luke pulled his hand out from under Alanna's – which wasn't really the same as holding hands – as she joined them at the booth. Jess gave her a wink, and Eve knew that Jess could tell pretty much exactly what she'd been thinking. She smiled, a real smile this time, signalling to Jess that everything was all good.

'There's coconut chocolate chip in there somewhere,' Luke said. He leaned closer to the gigantic sundae and poked around with his spoon a little. 'Got it.' He flicked the spoon through the whipped cream and butterscotch sauce, then held it out for Eve to take a bite.

'Yum. Thanks,' Eve told him. There was something so sexy about a boy feeding you ice cream.

'We were just talking about how you and Jess took down that demon yesterday,' Luke said.

'We're a good team,' Eve said, shooting a smile at Jess.

'How does it feel when you use your power?' Alanna's eyes were bright with curiosity. 'Does it hurt when the fire comes out?'

Alanna didn't seem to have any of the hostile vibes Eve had been expecting. Maybe she was getting over the fact that Eve had a natural ability to fight demons, while Alanna, a member of an ancient demon-hunting organization, didn't.

'It's weird.' Eve took another bite of ice cream. 'It's like . . . I know that it's hot. When I gather up the energy, it feels like a ball of lava in my chest. But even though I know that, it doesn't burn me. It's kind of hard to describe.'

'What do you mean, gather up the energy?' Alanna asked.

'The power is always in me,' Eve replied. 'It's like a current, running through my whole body. When I want to use it, I sort of concentrate and pull it all together right here.' She touched a spot near the centre of her rib cage.

'You should see her face when she lets the power go,' Jess commented. 'It's radiant. It's like she's been eating light.'

'It feels pretty amazing,' Eve added. 'I'm still not used to feeling so powerful. I was never a sporty kind of girl, not like Jess. But using the power almost makes me feel like an athlete, like I'm using my whole body.'

She hoped Alanna would report that back to Callum. Eve wanted the Order to know how strong she was and to remember that they were on the same side.

'Alanna, when the Order hears that Eve – and Jess – killed the latest demon, do you think it will make them more willing to share information with us?' Luke asked. 'I know *you* get that Eve should be part of any anti-demon plan, but do you think the rest of the Order will be convinced that there should be no more secrets from her?'

'I hope so,' Alanna answered. 'I'll do everything I can to bring them to that conclusion. Eve killing the demon they were worried about should remind them that she's stronger than anything we can create. Look what she did to the force field. It should also remind them that she's on our side – the side that kills demons.'

'Good.' Luke slid his arm around Eve and started playing with one of her long dark ringlets. She snuggled closer to him.

Alanna smiled. 'You two are a cute couple. I wondered when you'd get together.'

'Me too!' Jess exclaimed. 'I knew they lurrrved each other way before either of them did. At least before either of them would admit it.'

'Jess!' Eve cried, embarrassed. 'Nobody has said anything about anybody lurrrving anybody.' She shot a look at Luke, and he gave the ringlet wrapped around his fingers a tug.

'I've never heard of this lurrrve thing,' he said, grinning at her.

'Well, if you want to know what it is, it's how you feel right now, sitting there with Evie,' Jess told him. She looked over at Alanna. 'Can you believe how many months it took them to realize it?'

'It was pretty obvious to me,' Alanna answered. 'I don't know what their problem was.'

Eve was surprised. Alanna was actually treating Jess like a human being. Usually, she pretty much ignored her. Eve remembered what Luke had told her about Alanna thinking the Order had been wrong to put up the barrier. Maybe that made her feel like all four of them were on the same side.

'Can I ask another question about your power?' Alanna said to Eve. 'I'm not trying to drive you crazy, it's just that . . .' Alanna gave a little shrug, the roses on her shoulder tattoo rippling as if a breeze had passed by them. 'It's just that I've never met anyone who had anything like your abilities. And since I'm all about killing demons too, I'm really curious.'

'It's OK. Ask,' Eve told her.

'Is it basically limitless?' Alanna asked. 'If you had to fight a bunch of demons in a row, would your power still be as hot?'

Eve shook her head. 'It runs out. Well, not completely out. I can always feel a little spark of it inside. But I can only use it for so long at one time, then I need to recharge.'

'It used to be that time was the only way for Eve's power to build up,' Luke added. 'But when we were going after Amunnic, she realized that she could absorb electricity and use it to recharge. She blacked out the whole town the first time she did it.' He flicked the maraschino cherry off the rocky-road ice cream, and then scooped up a bite.

Eve reached over and plucked the cherry up by the stem, then popped it into her mouth. 'You want to know the real reason I got together with Luke?' she asked.

'I do,' Luke joked. 'I've been wondering.'

'Because he leaves all the cherries for me,' Eve said.

'Well . . . it's just because I hate them,' Luke confessed.

'You like them, she hates them, you're perfect together,' Jess said. 'You're like Jack Sprat and—' She was interrupted by her phone. She pulled it out of her bag.

'Hi, Mom,' she said, holding up one finger to show she'd be right back to the conversation.

Luke rolled another cherry over to the part of the sundae dish closest to Eve. Really, why *had* it taken them so long to get together? Something about him being a player and . . . It seemed so long ago that she'd had any doubts about him.

'*What?*' Jess cried. 'No!'

Eve snapped her head towards her best friend. All the blood was draining out of Jess's face, leaving her pale and scared-looking.

'I'll be right there, Mom.' Jess lurched to her feet, knocking against Alanna.

'Jess, what's going on?' Eve asked.

'I have to get home right now,' Jess told her. 'Something horrible has happened!'

Jess bolted up the stairs towards her bedroom so fast that Eve could hardly keep up. Luke and Alanna were only a few steps behind.

'I came in to put away some laundry, and that's when I saw it. I don't know how it could have happened.' Jess's mom sat on the bed, holding the beautiful new Dolce & Gabbana dress in her lap. 'I can't imagine who would do something like this.'

'Let me see.' Jess took the dress from her mother and shook it out. She held it up in front of her and turned to face the mirror over her dresser.

Eve gasped. The gown had been slashed in three places, the delicate chiffon hanging in shreds. 'Oh, Jess. That's awful. I can't believe this,' she cried. Who could have done something like that? And to Jess. Jess was one of those people who made friends with pretty much everyone she met.

Tears began to slide down Jess's cheeks. 'We'll get you another dress,' her mother promised.

'I don't want another dress. I want this dress.' Jess slid her finger into one of the slashes. Eve could see that her hand was trembling.

'Maybe we can find another one,' Eve suggested. 'I know that it's an original, but maybe we could find something in the same style.'

Jess shook her head. 'I couldn't wear anything like it. If I did, I'd just be seeing this one.' She gently laid the dress on her bed.

'I'll let you be with your friends,' Mrs Meredith said gently. 'But call me if you want me. I'll be right downstairs.' She gave Jess a hug before she left the room.

'Someone sneaked into my room and did this.' Jess sank down onto the floor and leaned against the bed. 'Someone came right into my room.'

Eve sat down next to her. She and Jess had had so much fun in this room, watching movies, telling secrets, getting ready for parties. Now, suddenly, it didn't feel like the same place. 'It's going to be OK,' she said. 'You're still going to the prom – the Senior Prom – with Seth. That's what matters.'

'Who could hate me enough to do this?' Jess asked, without looking at Eve. She stared straight ahead, eyes wide, as if she were watching her dress be destroyed again and again.

Luke sat across from her. A second later, Alanna joined them on the floor.

'Jess, I think we have a pretty good idea who did this,' Luke said.

'You do?' Alanna exclaimed. 'Who? Is there something the Order should know about?'

'Simon . . .' Eve breathed. She hadn't even thought about him until Luke spoke. But he'd been skulking around Jess's house, and watching her during school, and he'd written her that horrible letter.

'Jess turned this guy Simon down when he invited her to the prom,' Luke explained to Alanna. 'He didn't handle it very well.'

'I guess not.' Alanna glanced over at the dress.

'I think he might have cursed me.' Jess blinked a few times. 'Eve and I saw him with this book. It had all these weird markings on the front. Not letters. It could have been a book of spells.'

'What do you know about this guy? Is it possible he's practising the dark arts?' Alanna asked. Only someone from the Order would treat Jess's idea about being cursed so seriously.

'I know it's Deepdene. And I know weird things happen here pretty much on a daily basis,' Luke said. 'But I don't think we should jump to the conclusion that there's something supernatural going on. To me it seems like Simon was obsessing about Jess, without her even realizing it. Then when she turned him down, he lost it.'

'I'm so used to looking for paranormal answers, I just went there,' Alanna told them. 'But what Luke said makes sense, not that I know the guy. This Simon gets mad that you won't go to the prom with him, so he cuts up your dress.'

Eve sprang to her feet. 'It was him. It has to have been him.' She began to pace, her power roiling inside her. Her best friend was being terrorized. Eve wasn't going to let it continue. It was stopping now.

The fingers on her right hand twitched, and before she could stop it, a small bolt of lightning escaped. It flew towards the bed, and ripped into Jess's dress with a sizzle. The scent of scorched fabric filled the room.

'Oh, Jess, I'm so sorry. So, so sorry,' Eve cried. She dropped down next to Jess and wrapped her arm around Jess's shoulders. 'I just got so angry thinking about Simon that . . . It just burst out.'

'It's OK. It was already ruined.' Jess's voice was flat and emotionless.

'Luke, do you think . . . ?' Eve nodded towards the door. Jess needed her right now, but she didn't need a crowd.

'Alanna, you wanted to see the animal bodies I found in the woods. I can walk you out there now,' Luke offered.

'Thanks,' Eve mouthed, then turned her attention back to Jess, trying to think of anything that could possibly make her feel better. This was way beyond the powers of chocolate.

'What's that?' Alanna pointed to the strip of scorched earth running through the woods. 'Was there some kind of fire?'

Luke hesitated, but decided to tell her the truth. 'Eve's power made it,' he answered. He looked at her face, trying to judge her reaction. When he'd first seen what Eve's out-of-control power had done, it had turned his whole body cold.

Alanna crouched down and ran her fingers over part of the charred area, her face giving no clue to what she was thinking. She turned her gaze from the ground to the trees. 'Is that what happed up there too, those bare spots?'

Luke nodded. He hated even looking at the trees Eve had zapped.

'Was she fighting the demon? I thought it was over by Jess's house,' Alanna said as she stood up.

'It was.' He struggled to decide how to describe what had happened. 'Eve had just found out that the Order had put up the force field without telling her. She was devastated – and furious. Basically, she just lost it. She ran out here and this is what happened.' He swept out a hand, indicating the ground and trees. 'Then, when she got to the barrier, she threw her power at it until she blasted through.'

'This wasn't a momentary loss of control, like what we just saw at Jess's,' Alanna commented. 'This is major destruction.'

'I was just glad she had the sense to get herself away from people,' Luke admitted. He didn't like talking behind Eve's back. But he was worried about her slips in control.

'Does that happen a lot, where her powers are in charge of her instead of the other way around?' Alanna asked.

'It used to happen more at the beginning, when she first got her power,' Luke replied. 'But not really since then. It was mostly because she got mad. Emotion made it hard for her to keep a grip.'

'Still does, it seems to me,' Alanna said. 'Back there with Jess, it was clear that Eve was upset.'

'She and Jess are really good friends,' Luke explained, feeling protective. 'And what Simon did – it had to be him – was really horrible. That's why she lost it.'

Alanna pursed her lips, as if trying to decide what to say. 'Luke, you have to remember that Eve isn't completely human. She might never be able to fully control the demon part of her nature.'

'Eve is as human as me or you. Having that demon blood is what gave her and the other Deepdene Witches their power. And she uses that power to fight demons,' Luke protested. 'OK, occasionally she lets her power slip, but before this it had been months. She just got especially upset. And who could blame her, given what the Order did? They could've killed her!'

'There are always going to be things that upset her. There's no avoiding it.' Alanna's brows came together in a frown. 'It's possible the demon part of her is getting stronger and that's why she isn't able to keep her power in check the way she used to. If that's true, it will keep happening. And the results might be a lot more serious than some burned-up grass and a scorched dress.'

'You make it sound like her power is a bad thing,' Luke said. 'Eve uses it to fight evil. She uses it to kill demons. She wouldn't be doing that if even a small part of her was demonic.' He wanted to believe that. He *did* believe it most of the time. But the way Eve had let her power explode here in the woods disturbed him. If she hadn't made it here, if she'd lost control on Main Street . . .

Luke didn't want to think about that, but he wasn't able to push the idea away completely.

'I understand that you want to see her as human, Luke, but she's not. You have to face that. It's dangerous for you if you don't. Demon blood makes her part demon. That's simply a fact. Maybe her human side will always be dominant, but that doesn't mean the demon side isn't there.' Alanna took his hand and gave it a squeeze. 'I'm going to tell you something that I'm not supposed to,' she said. 'And it's partly because I'm afraid for you – you and Jess.'

Luke locked eyes with her. 'What?'

'The Order is very concerned that Eve blasted down the force field. The reason they put it up in the first place is because they wanted to observe Eve in a contained environment, where any damage she did would be limited,' Alanna explained. 'That's why I'm really here. They sent me to investigate. I'm supposed to determine if Eve can be trusted – or if she's a threat.'

Chapter Nine

Luke followed his torch beam deeper into the woods, comforted by the feel of his sword strapped to his back. He wanted to take another look at the dead animals. There had to be something he'd missed. Some clue that would help him figure out what was going on.

He followed the course of Eve's fire. It was the easiest way for him to find the unmarked border between his town and East Hampton. The damage looked worse at night. So many bare branches twisted up into the moonlight. Luke hadn't remembered so many leaves being destroyed. And wasn't the path of scorched grass wider than before?

Suddenly he was aware of the beating of his heart. Hard, shuddering thuds, as if his heart was trying to escape from his body. Cold sweat began pumping from his pores and slithering down his back. His body was telling him something was very wrong. It was telling him to go back, to run back to the safety of the town, the rectory, his bed.

It took all his will, but Luke continued down the dark path. He felt the presence of evil around him, heavy and smothering, stronger than anything he'd felt during a demon battle. What was out here?

He reached behind him to touch the sword. His blood ran cold. The sheath was still strapped to his back, but the sword was gone. How was that possible? It couldn't have fallen out of the sheath. Should he turn back and look for it? He would need it soon, if his instincts were right. He should—

A shriek, long and saturated with pain, dragged him away from his thoughts. Luke did the only thing he could – he ran towards it.

His torch beam found Eve at the end of the scorched path. Relief surged through him. He wouldn't have to fight whatever was out here alone. A moment later, he realized that Eve was in a long white nightgown, and it was spattered with blood. She swayed on her feet, her face pale, so pale.

'Where are you hurt?' he exclaimed as he rushed towards her. Something caught his foot, and he fell to the ground, the taste of ashes filling his mouth. He struggled to stand, but he couldn't pull his foot free.

He twisted round to see what had caught him – and he screamed. The scream felt like it was ripping and tearing his body as it surged out of him.

A hand. A hand grasped Luke's foot. Jess's hand. Her throat had been slit. Blood gurgled from the wound when she spoke. 'Stop her. You have to kill her.' Jess's eyes went blank, her soul slipping away.

Luke jerked his foot free from her grasp and leaped to his feet. Two more bodies lay between him and Eve. Throats slit, eyes staring up at him.

'Eve, what have you done?'

She smiled at him, and he could see spatters of blood on her teeth. 'I've been killing demons, Pooh Bear.' She pulled the sword, the sword Payne had entrusted him with, from behind her back. 'This town is full of them.'

Luke stumbled backwards, but before he could turn and run, Eve was on him. The slash down his throat didn't hurt, but he could feel his hot blood, his *life*, gushing out of him.

'Nooo!' he shouted.

And then he jerked upright in bed.

In bed. He'd been dreaming. He pressed both hands against his throat. Damp with sweat, but that was all.

Luke lay still for a moment, his heart still racing. Then he got up slowly, his eyes adjusting to the darkness in the room. No way was he going back to sleep now. He might never go back to sleep for the rest of his life.

He sat down at his computer, taking a deep breath. Eve's face smiled at him from the screensaver. He reached out and traced the line of her cheek with his finger. This was the real Eve, smiling, full of strength and righteousness. The girl who had killed demon after demon.

He shuddered, remembering the words of the dream Eve. 'I'm killing demons,' she'd said, with the bodies of their friends lying around her.

'I talked to Seth last night about the dress,' Jess told Eve the next morning. They stood in front of the school finishing up their coffees from Java Nation. Star-shaped silver flyers for the prom had been tacked to some of the trees, and they fluttered gently in the light breeze. 'He was so furious. He's positive Simon did it.'

'It's really the only thing that makes sense,' Eve answered. She'd thought about it a lot. She hadn't been able to stop herself. But all the scenarios she came up with had ended up involving Simon.

'At least the house won't be empty today. Peter has the flu and mom decided to keep him home,' Jess said. 'He's been pretty out of it, but he'll hear if anyone tries to get in.'

'Have you been able to figure out if he saw us with' – Eve did a check to make sure no one was in hearing range – 'the squishy demon?'

'I didn't come right out and ask him, because if he hadn't seen anything, I didn't want him to know there'd been anything to see,' Jess replied. 'But I made sure to talk to him once I got cleaned up. I'm almost positive he would have said something to me.' She finished her last sip of coffee, then crumpled the paper cup. 'You ready to go in?'

Eve glanced at her watch. Almost fifteen minutes before homeroom. 'I want to stay here and keep an eye out for Simon. I want to at least ask him some questions.'

'How will that do any good? He's not going to say "Yes, I sneaked into Jess's house and went at her dress with a knife,"' Jess pointed out.

'Maybe I won't ask any questions then. Maybe I'll just—' Eve stuck out her hands and wiggled her fingers.

Jess grabbed her by the wrists and pulled Eve's hands down. 'You wouldn't do that! Would you?'

'Of course not! I was joking.' Eve shook her head. How could Jess even ask her such a thing? 'Simon is a person. Probably a sick, deranged person, but a person. I'd never use my zap on someone who wasn't a demon.'

Jess gave an apologetic smile. 'I guess I was thinking of the way your power shot out at the dress yesterday.'

'I got so furious. I didn't mean to do it. It just happened,' Eve explained. 'I'm so sorry. I know it was already ruined, but I hate that I did that to your beautiful, beautiful prom dress.'

'I know. I think you were as upset about the dress as I was. That's because you're a true friend,' Jess said. 'But if we talk to Simon, stay calm, OK? Maybe there are some breathing techniques you could use. My mom is all about the breathing techniques.'

'I'll be OK. It was just the shock of seeing your dress, I think. And realizing Simon had been in your house. In your room. It made me a little crazy. But it won't be like that today. I've had a little time to process it.' Eve finished her coffee. 'What about you? How're you doing now? Have you thought more about what you want to do for a dress? Are you sure you don't want to find something sort of like it. Maybe something chiffon at least?'

'No. I'd just keep thinking about the first one,' Jess said. 'But we need to get to Manhattan soon. There's not much time left to shop.'

'It's a good thing I busted down the Order's force field, then,' Eve said. 'Otherwise I wouldn't be able to go to Manhattan with you – or anywhere else, for that matter.'

Jess clapped her hand over her mouth. 'You know, I never even thought about that! How dare they try to keep my prom adviser trapped here?'

Eve smiled. 'Well, their barrier wasn't strong enough to keep me trapped! We'll go to the city, and we'll find you an even more perfect perfect dress,' she promised. 'And I won't call dibbies even once.'

Jess shook her finger at Eve with a mock scowl. 'You better not, missy.'

Eve kept the smile on her face, but it wasn't too easy. She still thought she'd been completely within her dibbies rights when she'd called them the last time.

Jess's teasing smile faded and she wrapped her arms around herself. 'Here comes Simon.' He was cutting across the front lawn of the school, head down, his usual big leather book under his arm.

'Do you want to talk to him with me?' Eve asked. 'You don't have to. I'm fine doing it by myself. Although I bet Luke would want to come with me, just cause—'

'Cause he's a boy,' Jess finished for her. 'That's a good idea. Wait and do it with Luke.'

'Uh-oh. Someone's going to beat me to it,' Eve said, gasping as Seth's Escalade lurched up onto the sidewalk and came to a stop. The head of every person in the quad turned towards the sound of the squealing brakes.

A second later, Seth and Dave jumped out of the SUV. They were on Simon before he even had time to turn round.

'Seth, no!' Jess shouted. Seth already had Simon pinned to the ground, his fist poised to slam into the other boy's face.

Eve and Jess rushed over to the melee. A small circle of spectators had already formed around them. Eve wasn't sure how they were supposed to break up a fight involving two big guys – without the zap – but they had to try. Or was there a teacher around? She scanned the area. Nope. Never around when you needed them. But maybe someone would report the fight to the office.

'I'm sorry I sent the letter,' Simon cried. 'I was going to tell Jess that. I waited at her house, but she wouldn't talk to me.'

'That's why you were at my house?' Jess exclaimed.

'You slashed up her prom dress, you little freak. You're giving Jess the money for it, and you're never going to so much as look at her again!' Seth yelled. He started to deliver the punch, but Jess grabbed his arm in both hands.

'No!' she told him. 'We don't know he did anything. Not for sure.'

'Who else would have gone into your room and slashed up your dress?' Seth demanded. 'He did it because he was pissed off that you turned him down.'

'No I didn't! I don't even know what you're talking about. What dress? What do you think I did?' Simon blurted out, his words tripping over each other because he was speaking so fast. He sounded sincere to Eve. But she agreed with Seth. Simon was the only person who had a reason to destroy Jess's prom dress.

'Leave him alone, Seth,' Jess begged.

'Smash his head in!' Dave called at the same time.

'I won't go to the prom with you if you touch him. Are you listening?' Jess shouted. 'Are you hearing me?'

'Yeah.' Seth opened his fist, getting a few 'boo's from the crowd, and Jess let go of his arm. 'I know what you did,' he told Simon. 'Stay out of my way. And stay away from Jess,' he ordered. Then he jerked his chin at Dave and they both started towards the Escalade.

Seth looked over his shoulder. 'Come on, Jess.' Jess shook her head, not moving from her spot next to Eve. 'Whatever,' he muttered as he got in the SUV.

Simon scrambled to his feet, his face pale. Eve picked up his book, squinting down at the dusty leather binding. 'What is this, anyway?' she asked, running her fingers over the symbols on the front. They looked strange, but they couldn't be demon runes. If they were, she knew she'd be able to read them.

'It's a textbook for Russian,' Simon muttered, taking it from her. 'My dad's making me take an accelerated course this summer, and I'm trying to get a head start.' He turned to Jess, but he kept his eyes on the ground instead of her face. 'I am sorry about the letter. I was a jerk. I'm sorry. That's why I was at your house. I just wanted to tell you that.'

He began to walk away, then suddenly turned back. This time he looked Jess right in the eye. 'I really don't know what he was talking about. With the dress, I mean.'

Eve chewed on her lip and watched him as he walked back towards the school. It really did sound like he was telling the truth.

'I kind of believe him,' Jess said.

'I kind of believe him too,' Eve admitted. 'But if he's telling the truth, then who slashed up your prom dress?'

'Type in . . . warm Jell-O demon,' Eve suggested to Luke.

'Rotten-fish-smelling, shoe-destroying, warm Jell-O demon,' Jess amended.

Luke tapped his fingers impatiently on the keyboard of Eve's laptop while the girls lounged on Eve's bed. He was trying to research the demon Eve and Jess had fought the other day, so he could update his database. But the girls were not being helpful. 'Can you focus a little?' he asked, trying not to sound irritated.

Eve flopped back on her bed. 'Come on, Luke, we just got out of school. And it was a crazy day with Seth almost pounding Simon into the ground. We need a break.' She nodded her head towards Jess. Luke got that Jess had had a hard day, but they still needed to research the latest demon.

'Yeah, that was scary. I thought I might have to break out my kung fu on Seth to get him to back off,' Jess said. 'I keep thinking about Simon's face when he said he didn't know what Seth was talking about. If he was lying, he should join the drama club immediately.'

'Which means we have no idea who destroyed your dress,' Luke said.

'I can't think about that. Not right now. My head will implode.' Jess flopped back next to Eve. 'Right now, me need fun.'

'Fuuuun,' Eve groaned, like she was Frankenstein's monster.

'Fuuuun,' Jess groaned back with a monster voice.

Luke gave a regular groan. They were making him insane. He was trying to discuss a demon here. A demon! 'That thing was in our town,' Luke reminded them from his seat at Eve's desk. 'What if it had stumbled across someone else? Someone with no power or kung-fu training.' He leaned forward, looking back and forth between Eve and Jess. 'I need you both to get serious. What else do we know about the demon?'

Eve raised her hand, waving it like an over-eager student. 'I know something!'

She made him ask. 'What?' Luke said.

'The demon? It's dead!' she answered.

'And that's all we really need to know,' Jess chimed in.

'No, it's not,' Luke snapped. 'What if it turns out that the demon can reconstruct itself? Maybe the puddle of goo returned to demon form as soon as it hit the sewer. Or maybe this kind of demon travels in packs. For all we know, a demon could have been in Jess's house, slashing up her prom dress. Somebody had to have done it, and it doesn't seem like Simon is such a likely choice any more.'

'Especially not now that we found out the spell book is actually a Russian textbook,' Eve commented. 'Hey, remember that day on the phone when he said such weird-sounding words? He must have been speaking Russian!'

'You're right,' Jess said. 'Wow. It doesn't seem so creepy when I think of it that way.'

'No. Still strange, though,' Eve said. 'But more regular-strange. I mean, Simon-strange.' She looked over at Jess. 'Do you remember anything about how it sounded? Maybe we could look up the words somehow.'

Jess frowned. 'Not really. Maybe *atayka*? He talked so fast it was hard to make it out.' She pressed her fingers to her temples. 'Head beginning to implode.'

'Right. We weren't going to talk about Simon. Maybe we shouldn't talk about anything head-imploding at least for tonight.' Eve looked directly at Luke as she spoke. He got it. He knew she wanted him to drop the demon investigation.

He understood Jess needed to de-stress. But keeping the town safe was more important. They should both know that. 'There's still someone – or some*thing* – bad on the loose. We need to be ready,' he reminded them.

'If there's another demon, or if the first demon did pull its goopy self back together, we'll kill it again as soon as we see it,' Eve told him.

'Yeah, it only took a couple of minutes.' Jess frowned. 'Although it did ruin my beautiful pink sandals, and they were the cutest little shoes in North America.'

'No way,' Eve said. 'The cutest little shoes in North America are my black satin high tops with the blue laces. Your sandals might have been the prettiest little shoes on the east coast, though,' she added.

Luke shut his eyes for a long moment, trying to get

a grip on his temper. They were being so silly, as silly as kindergarten kids who hadn't had a nap. When he opened his eyes, he turned round and looked at Eve. 'You're the Deepdene Witch. You're responsible for the safety of everyone in the town. How can you be treating this so casually?'

Eve sat up, pushing her wildly curling hair away from her face. 'I'm not! I can't believe you even said that,' she snapped. 'It's just . . . it's been a nasty couple of days, with the Eve-killing barrier and the demon and Jess's dress. I thought we could all use a little while to chill. But if something bad happens, I'll be there. You know that.'

It was true. Eve always stepped up when there was an attack on the town. But she'd never acted so laid-back about her duty as the Deepdene Witch before. She was behaving as if it wasn't that big a deal that the lives of everyone who lived here depended on her.

Is it because her human side is being taken over by the demon side? That was a thought Luke didn't want to have, but he couldn't push it away. Maybe Alanna had been right. Was Eve changing? Was she going to turn into a threat to Deepdene herself?

'Why are you staring at me like that?' Eve asked him.

'I didn't realize I was staring,' he said, blood rushing to his face.

'That's probably because you're *always* staring at Eve,' Jess told him, with a wink.

Luke felt the back of his neck get hot, then his face. Did he walk around school in some kind of Eve daze that everyone could see?

'Look at him blush,' Jess cried.

Eve scooted to the end of the bed, then reached out and touched his face. 'I think it's sweet.'

'Blushing is not sweet, not in a guy.' Luke felt his face get hotter.

'Yeah, it is,' Eve told him. 'And so is staring, at least when it's you staring at me.'

'It's because you're so beautiful,' Luke said. It wasn't really a lie. She really was beautiful, and most of the time that was why he was staring at her.

She couldn't look like that and have something evil inside her. It was exactly what she had said – it had been a difficult few days and she and Jess wanted to blow off some steam. That didn't mean that she'd stopped caring about protecting people.

He felt his irritation draining away as turned back to the computer. Let them goof around. He'd keep working. He decided to do a search for demons that turned to liquid when they were killed. Assuming that the demon actually had been killed, which it probably had.

'Is this that book on the Deepdene Witch you were telling me about?' Luke heard Jess ask.

'Yeah, I found it on a secondhand-book website. A teeny, tiny publishing company did it way back in the eighteen-nineties,' Eve answered. 'You have to see my favourite illustration. It's a picture of the Deepdene Witch blasting a demon so hard that it got trapped inside a human body.'

Luke turned round. 'Let me see it too.'

'I thought you were working,' Eve teased him. She flipped through the small book, then held up a page for him and Jess to see.

Eve's great-great-great-grandmother had had the same long, curly hair that Eve did, at least as she was shown in the pen-and-ink drawing. That hair was whipped up around her face as she threw out lightning bolts from her fingers. Her expression reminded him of Eve's when she used her power – rapturous. Rapturous and fierce at the same time.

He turned his attention to the other girl in the drawing, the girl the Deepdene Witch was shooting the lightning at. She was writhing in pain, her face buried in her hands. Luke had to remind himself that the girl had been a demon, that the Witch wasn't torturing an innocent human.

'You think you could do that, Evie?' Jess asked. 'Zap a demon into a human body?'

'Maybe,' Eve said, closing the book and putting it back on her nightstand. 'Probably, since my great-great-great-grandmother could. But why would I want to? Wouldn't it always be better to just kill the demon?'

She said it in such a matter-of-fact way. Had killing really gotten so easy for Eve? Was it more than easy – was it exciting to her now? A thrill? Did part of her like it? The demon part?

'You're staring again,' Eve snapped. 'And don't say it's because I'm beautiful. Because the way you're staring is not how you stare at something beautiful.'

'Sorry.' Luke shook his head. 'I was just thinking about how much you've changed. When I first met you, you'd never have been able to talk about killing a demon that way, like it's just routine.'

'A lot has happened since we met,' Eve pointed out.

'I didn't even believe demons existed last summer,' Jess said.

'Yeah, but it sounded . . . It kind of sounded like

you were looking forward to it, the killing.' Luke tried to keep his voice neutral. He didn't want to accuse her of anything, but he was curious as to how she'd respond.

Eve's expression clouded over. 'First it's like I don't care enough about doing my Deepdene Witch duties. Now it's like I enjoy protecting the town too much. Make up your mind!' she exclaimed.

'Come on, Luke,' Jess said. 'There *is* something exciting about killing a demon. You know, getting in there and fighting evil. You've felt it too.'

Eve nodded. 'When you're using the sword in a demon battle, you're a warrior. Maybe you don't look forward to killing, but you want the demons dead. So do I.'

'Sorry,' Luke muttered. He didn't want to have a fight with her, not so soon after the last one. But it was more than that. He didn't want to fight with his girlfriend, sure, but more importantly, he didn't want Eve to lose her temper. Lately whenever she got mad, she got sparky. He didn't want to see what would happen this time.

'I think I know what the problem is,' Eve said. 'You're upset that Jess and I handled the demon without you. You don't want to feel like you and your famous demon-killing sword are unnecessary.'

'That's what you think?' Luke asked. *Unbelievable.*

'Yes, that's what I think,' Eve shot back. 'I think you'd rather have me be some damsel in distress that you could rescue.'

'There's a kung-fu class in about an hour I want to go to,' Jess put in, her voice a little too cheerful. She was probably embarrassed to be here when he and Eve were sort of arguing. 'Luke, come with me. We both need to keep building up our skills if we want to be able to back up Eve in a fight.'

'Oooh, I want to come too,' Eve exclaimed. 'I feel like kicking. Do you think I could split a board with my hand? Is that kung fu?'

Again, with the violence, Luke thought. When he first met Eve, she wouldn't have wanted to kick anything in case it messed up her toenail polish.

'No thanks, I'm going to go for a run,' Luke announced as he stood up. Running always helped him blast away his anger. 'It's obvious you two aren't going to help me with the research.'

'We *are* going to help,' Eve protested. 'We just wanted to relax for a while first.'

'You can do that without me,' Luke told her. 'See? I'm happy for you to take care of yourself.'

And I think we just had our second fight, he thought as he left the room. Maybe it was a good thing. Maybe he shouldn't even have a girlfriend who was half demon.

'Luke was in a mood this afternoon,' Eve commented as she and Jess headed to the kung-fu class.

Shanna and Rose waved at them from Shanna's porch. 'Jess, did you find a new dress yet?' Rose called.

Everyone knew that Jess's dress had been slashed. The fight – well, almost fight – between Seth and Simon had been big gossip, and the fact that Seth accused Simon of destroying Jess's gown was always part of the story.

'I have a couple of possibilities,' Jess answered as she and Eve walked partway across the lawn. 'I can go with one of them, but I'm hoping I find one I love as much as the first one. Eve and I are going to get in a power shopping trip to Manhattan.'

'And we *will* have success,' Eve added.

'Want to come hang? We made pomegranate lemonade,' Shanna said.

'Can't. We're going to *hi-yah* at kung-fu class,' Jess called. She gave a roundhouse kick to illustrate.

'Have fun!' Rose told them. Eve was glad she and

Jess had a reason not to stay and chat. Her head was too full of annoyance with Luke for her to be sociable.

'I mean, I know that demon research is important. But all we wanted was a little break,' she said as she and Jess continued walking.

Jess nodded. 'I'd say he qualified as a grumpy-pants.'

'It's like nothing I said was right. He kept picking at me.' Eve sighed. 'We almost had our second fight. Or did we have it? Did that qualify?'

'Well, he left in a huff,' Jess answered. 'But I think he left before you actually got to fight status.'

'That's something, I guess,' Eve said. 'Who knew that having a boyfriend would be such hard work?' Luke had been acting so weird, the way he had just been staring at her like she was a stranger or something.

'Seth actually gave me candy today,' Jess said. 'I think he was feeling guilty that some other guy had given me some when he hadn't. Even if the guy *was* a psycho stalker. Still, I thought it was cute of him.'

Eve felt a twinge of annoyance. She really didn't want to hear about a great boyfriend now, not when her own boyfriend had just left angry. Didn't Jess get that? 'That was nice of him,' was all she said.

'Speaking of nice – we haven't talked about Alanna yet. Did she get a personality make-over or something? At Ola's she actually acknowledged that I was at the table,' Jess said.

Eve was grateful for the subject change. 'I know. Usually she just focuses on Luke and acts like I'm in the way.'

'She still kinda focuses on Luke,' Jess commented.

Eve flashed on walking into Ola's and seeing Alanna leaning close to Luke, her hand on top of his. He shouldn't have let her do that, because, hello, he had a girlfriend. 'You're the one who's always telling me Alanna is too much older than Luke to be interested in him.'

Jess laughed. 'Maybe I've gotten more accepting of couples with an age difference, now that I'm with Seth.'

Eve couldn't believe Jess had just said that. Did she mean she was 'accepting' of Alanna and Luke?

Jess must have seen the outrage on Eve's face, because she immediately threw up her hands. 'I'm only kidding,' she quickly added.

'Seth actually is kind of old for you,' Eve commented. 'I mean, he'll be going off to college in the fall. And it's not like guys in college typically stay faithful to their high school girlfriends.' She wasn't entirely sure why she'd said that. She realized she was acting kind of bratty. But still, it was true. Everyone knew couples hardly ever stayed together when one person went off to college. 'At least you'll get the Senior Prom out of it.'

'You are so jealous that I'm going to the prom,' Jess burst out. 'Just admit it!'

'Why would I be jealous?' Eve shot back. 'I'm with Luke. I don't care if he's a freshman like me. He's great.'

'So great you've had two fights with him in about two minutes,' Jess said.

'You just said it wasn't a fight!' Eve cried. They were almost at Main Street. She told herself to keep her voice down. She didn't want to make a scene and have everyone talking about it at school tomorrow.

'I was being nice!' Jess exclaimed. 'You should try it sometime!'

'What is that even supposed to mean?' Eve was genuinely baffled. She was never not nice to Jess. Well, until right now.

'Trying to call dibbies when we were shopping for my prom dress? That was so selfish, Eve! You really can't stand that I'm going to the prom and you're not.' Jess's face was flushed with anger.

Eve stopped walking and turned to face her best friend. 'You're the jealous one! You can learn all the kung-fu you want, but you'll never have powers like I do. Never!'

'I'm going home,' Jess announced. 'I can't stand to be near you for another second.' She whirled round and rushed away.

Eve stared after her. She wasn't sure what had happened with Luke, but *that* had definitely been a fight. And it had been all Jess's fault!

Luke pulled off his T-shirt as soon as he walked into his room. It had been stuck to his body with sweat. He'd just run farther than he ever had before, until his legs ached and his lungs burned. It hadn't helped. He was still frustrated that Eve and Jess had blown off the demon research.

And he was still bothered by the changes he was seeing in Eve. She'd had demon blood when he first met her – obviously she was born with that. But her powers had only just started to manifest back then. Maybe Alanna was right: as the powers grew stronger, the demon side of her grew stronger too.

Or maybe Luke was just overreacting to that

nightmare he'd had last night. He was never going to be able to forget it.

He needed to shower. Badly. But he wanted to rest for at least a couple of minutes first. He pulled up his blinds and opened his window. The breeze floating in off the ocean would feel good right now.

Wait, he thought as he dropped down on the bed. *That's not right.*

He'd left the blinds up this morning, he was sure of it. Why had they been shut? His dad wouldn't have done it. He mostly stayed out of Luke's room. He always joked that Luke deserved a private man-cave. Not that he'd provided the very large flat screen TV that any man-cave should have.

Someone had been in the room, though. Luke sat up and glanced around. Now that he was paying attention, he kept noticing other things that were off. A book that he was sure had been on the right side of his desk was now on the left. And a couple of pages of his history paper had ended up on the floor.

A demon had gone right into Jess's room. At least Luke was pretty sure it had been a demon, since the girls had decided that Simon was innocent. Had a demon been in his room too?

The sword!

Could a demon have come in and stolen it? Luke jumped up. He'd stashed the sword under his bed after he'd gotten it out to fight Amunnic. He pulled up the bedspread and peered into the dimness beneath the bed.

There was nothing there but a few fluffy clumps of dust. The sword was gone. It was ancient and rare and incredibly valuable. It was the only weapon that could kill a demon. That Payne had given it to Luke with his dying breath made it even more precious. And now it was gone.

Luke let the bedspread drop. As he did, he noticed something sparkling in the sunlight. He bent over to check it out, and found that one of Eve's earrings had gotten caught on the cloth of the bedspread. He pulled it off and studied it. Long and dangly. Eve wore earrings like that a lot.

But so did a lot of girls. Lots and lots of girls. Lots and lots of girls hadn't been in his room though.

He fingered the delicate silver earring. It couldn't have been caught on his bedspread for long. He would have noticed it.

Which meant that Eve – or at least some girl – must have been in his room. Recently. While he wasn't home. But who? And why?

Chapter Ten

Oooh, Eve thought as she stepped into the Deepdene High gym before school the next morning. A glittering silver Eiffel Tower about four metres tall stood in one corner. A three-metre-tall Arc de Triomphe, also silver, stood near the entrance. They looked like they'd been brushed with moonlight, which was perfect for the theme of the prom – An Evening in Paris.

Students, mostly seniors, were clustered in groups working to continue the gym's transformation. Carrie, Lindsey and a couple of others were painting a huge moon, Dave and some guys from the basketball team were weaving twinkle lights around the bases of the flower displays, Jess was in a group adding glitter to what looked like at least a hundred stars.

Eve's stomach started doing gymnastics when she spotted Jess at the star station. Should she go over and apologize? No. The fight was a lot more Jess's fault than Eve's, and Jess was the one who'd stomped off. If someone was going to apologize, it should be her.

And anyway, Eve was kind of apologizing just by being here. She didn't have to help decorate. That was a job for people who were going to the prom. Eve thought joining in would show Jess that she was absolutely wrong about Eve being jealous of her going to the dance. OK, maybe she'd been a little jealous, but she hadn't acted jealous, so that didn't count. Besides, she'd mostly been jealous of Jess going to the prom without her, not of her actually going.

She took a deep breath, let it out slowly, and walked over to the table where Jess and the others were working. She gave Jess a tentative smile as she picked up a star and a glue stick. Jess didn't smile back, and Eve was almost positive that Jess had seen her.

Her heart squeezed. She and Jess had never had a fight that had lasted overnight. They hardly ever got in fights at all, and if they did have a disagreement, they got over it in a few hours. She shot another look at Jess. Jess was staring at the star she was working on like she was performing life or death surgery.

Eve began running her glue stuck over one section of the 3D star. When she finished, she sprinkled the section with silver glitter. *Why am I standing here doing this? Jess clearly doesn't want me here.* But Eve couldn't walk away. If she stayed, maybe Jess would get that Eve wanted her prom to be special. And that she owed Eve an apology.

'Jess!'

Eve looked over her shoulder. It was Peter. Had Jess told him about the fight? She got busy spreading glue over another piece of the star, deciding to wait and see how he acted towards her.

'Jess, Mom told me to give this to you.' Out of the corner of her eye, Eve saw Peter thrust a sheet of paper at his sister. 'Permission slip or something.'

'Thanks,' Jess told him. She glanced at the clock. 'You'd better hurry if you're going to make it over to the middle school in time.'

'Mom gave me a note in case I ended up being late. I think it might have taken me a while to find you,' he answered cheekily. 'I might have had to check Java Nation, where I might have had to buy a cinnamon scone so I'd have the energy to keep looking.'

'Get out of here,' Jess told him, but she was smiling, and her voice was full of affection.

'I'm going, I'm going,' Peter told Jess. Then he glanced over at Eve and smiled. 'Did you find what you were looking for the other day, Eve?' he asked.

'What? When?' Eve didn't know what he was talking about.

'Monday. You said you had to find something in Jess's room,' Peter said.

'Monday! This Monday?' Jess exclaimed.

'I wasn't at your house on Monday,' Eve told him. 'You must be thinking about one of the times I was over with Jess.'

'No, it was definitely Monday. I remember I was starting to feel sick, and I stayed home Tuesday. I don't know where you were when she came by, Jess,' Peter replied. He gave a shrug. 'OK, I'm heading out. If I'm too late, the note won't cover me. But I think I have time for one of those doughnuts.' He headed for the snack table that had been set up near the benches.

'You were at my house after school on Monday?' Jess burst out. She was looking at Eve now, her eyes blazing.

'Uh, no. I don't know why he said that. I was with you on Monday, remember? At Ola's,' Eve replied.

'You said you had to go back to school to turn in a report. You had time to get to my house before you showed up at Ola's.'

'Huh?' Eve said. 'Why would I do that?'

'I knew you were jealous, but I never thought you'd do something so horrible. Never!' Jess cried.

It took Eve a second to get it, just because it was so outrageous. 'Wait. You think I went to your house and destroyed your dress?' she yelped. 'That's insane.'

'My dress was fine when I left for school on Monday. Then, right after you were at my house, it was shredded,' Jess shot back.

'I didn't go to your house. I came back to school to give in my history report.' Eve's fingers began to tingle. She curled her hands into fists, crushing the paper star she still held. She wasn't going to let her power loose now, in front of everyone.

'Of course you'd lie about it,' Jess snapped.

Half the people in the gym were listening, although some of them were pretending not to. But Eve didn't care about any of them. She only cared about Jess. 'Jess, you're my best friend. Why would I do that?'

'Because you're jealous. You're so jealous I get to go to the prom and you don't!' Jess yelled.

'I'm here, aren't I? I'm helping decorate, because I want the prom to be perfect for you and Seth.' Eve tried to keep her voice steady and calm so Jess would really listen to her words.

'I didn't ask you to help. This is supposed to be for

people going to the prom. Which is why you're here, shoving your way in,' Jess snapped.

Tremors ripped up and down Eve's body, her power raging. 'Fine. I'm leaving.' She turned and rushed towards the door. She was moving so fast that she almost ran into Luke, on his way in.

'I'm so glad you're here!' she told him. All she wanted was to feel his arms around her, but when she reached out, he stepped away from her. Stung, Eve let her arms drop to her sides, the hot tremors of power increasing. 'What's wrong? Are you still mad that I didn't feel like researching yesterday? I just—'

Luke didn't say anything. He just held up one of her silver earrings, the one with a long dangly chain of linked hearts. 'Where d'you find that?' she asked.

'So it is yours,' he said.

'Uh-huh. I didn't even realize I'd lost it. Where did you find it?' she asked again.

'Where do you think?' he retorted, and his voice was like ice, hard and cold.

'I don't know. That's why I asked you.' What was with him? Him *and* Jess. Eve still could hardly believe that Jess thought Eve slashed her dress. How could her best friend believe such a thing? How could her boyfriend be looking at her with such coldness in his eyes?

Anger began to burn inside her, and Eve felt her power racing, racing, racing. It wanted out.

'I can't stay in here,' she gasped. 'I need out.'

She'd only managed to take one step when the sound of shattering glass filled the gym. Eve whirled towards the sound, staring in astonishment at the birds smashing through the big windows high in the walls. Eve was hit with so many different impressions so fast, it was hard to take them all in. Safety glass raining down on the prom decorators. A lot of birds. Black. Huge. With wrinkled faces and dripping folds of flesh. Vultures.

They hissed as they began circling the room. Green bile dripped from their curved beaks. Their eyes glowed yellow and had no pupils.

They're not regular vultures, Eve realized. *They're demons.*

'Luke, get everyone out!' Eve yelled. People were scrambling for the doors, and the exit was already jammed. 'Jess! Help Luke get this place cleared. I'll deal with the rest.'

'OK. I'm calling Alanna too,' Luke announced as he headed for the side doors.

Alanna. Didn't he even trust Eve to handle it? She was the one with demon-fighting powers, not Alanna.

Her power didn't need any time to rev. It was right there waiting. Eve chose one of the demon birds as a target, then thrust her hands out at it. Her lightning flew from her fingers – straight and fast. The creature gave a shrill squawk, and Eve could smell singed feathers.

The demon wheeled in the air, then dived at Eve. Another demon vulture came at her from the other side. Eve aimed one hand at each and threw her power at them. She got the first one again and it plummeted, hitting the wooden floor of the gym with a dull thud. 'Got you! Yeah!' Eve shouted. All that anger she'd been feeling had a place to go now. It felt good to let her power fly at the demons.

The other demon bird kept coming at Eve, raking her arm with its talons and then zooming away before she could blast it again. Eve felt the scratches like hot lines of fire in her flesh, but she didn't have time to think about that.

The sound of hissing grew louder, and Eve saw that more vultures were streaming in through the windows. The air above her was a mass of swirling black. It felt like the birds had sucked all the oxygen out of the air.

'Peter, come on!' she heard Jess yell. 'You can't stay

here.' Eve spotted her over by the doughnut table, trying to pull her brother to his feet. But he stayed crouched on the gym floor, using both arms to protect his face. Eve wanted to race over to him and Jess, but she knew the best way she could help them was to deal with the demons.

This time, Eve didn't bother aiming. She focused on her power, and when the bolts slammed from her fingers, she managed to keep them connected to her. She flung her hands over her head and it was as if she was controlling two zigzagging lasers.

Eve spun in a circle, hitting as many birds as she could, pushing the power out so hard that the long bolts of light cracked and spit sparks. A few birds dropped to the floor. One struggled to stay aloft with most of the feathers burned off one wing.

The other demons retaliated. They swooped down at her, one after the other. Eve curved her arms over her head as they attacked with their talons and beaks, biting and scratching as if they planned to strip off her skin bit by bit.

And they would if she didn't fight back. Blood was already streaming down her arms, soaking into her hair. At least the adrenaline rush was keeping her from really feeling the pain. Eve kept one arm around her head, and gave short lightning blasts with the free hand. Methodically. Blasting at one bird until it went down, then moving on, trying to ignore the pain of the continuous jabs and rips from the other demons.

There's only five of them now, that's all, she told herself. She aimed, fired. *Four left, just four.*

When she had gotten the demon count down to two, her head jerked back suddenly. One of the creatures had managed to tangle a talon in her hair and tear a clump free. Eve spun and used both hands to zap it. While she was attacking it, the last of the demon vultures, the biggest one, closed in on her. It pinched a piece of her upper arm in its beak. It shook its head like a dog with a bone, and Eve's arm jerked, sending her power shooting wildly across the gym.

The bird wouldn't release her arm. Fine. She'd use that. She grabbed it with one hand and let her power fly directly from her fingers into its body.

The last demon exploded. So did the dead creatures at her feet. Black feathers and bloody pieces of wrinkled flesh flew into the air.

It's over, Eve thought as the feathers began to slowly drift back down. *I did it!* She'd taken them all on – and won. She pushed her long hair away from her face and a couple of fingers came back wet and red with blood from the spot where the bird had yanked out her hair. Her body was hurting in too many places to register, but she was OK.

She surveyed the gym. Pretty much everyone had made it out. Jess was crouched next to Peter. Luke and Alanna were standing blocking the closed doors of the main entrance. Eve hadn't noticed when Alanna showed up. It must have been pretty fast, though. The whole battle had only lasted minutes, even though it had felt endless. Was Alanna keeping tabs on Eve? Was that why she'd managed to get here within minutes of Luke calling her?

That didn't matter right now. Eve rushed towards Peter and Jess. 'Is he OK?'

'How could you do that to him?' Jess demanded. Peter had his head buried in his hands.

'I zapped him?' Eve cried, horrified. The back of his shirt had a large burned spot, but the skin below it looked unharmed. Relief flooded through Eve. Her power had always had a different effect on humans. She'd even managed to heal some people after the demon Malphus had made them insane. But she'd never zapped a non-demon before.

'I didn't mean to,' she said. 'There were so many of

them coming at me. And one really latched on to my arm and yanked. That must be when I hit him.' Eve touched the spot gingerly. It still hurt. 'I was aiming at the bird, but when my arm moved, the shot went wild. I didn't know it got Peter.'

Jess didn't answer. She just stared at Eve as though she'd never seen her before.

Eve felt a cold pit settle in her stomach. 'You don't think I did it on purpose, do you?'

'I don't know what to think,' Jess told her. 'If you'd asked me last week whether you could have ruined my prom dress, I would have said no way. Clearly, I don't know you like I thought I did.'

'I *didn't*—' Eve began.

Luke strode over, interrupting her. 'Why did you take the sword? If I'd had it, I could have at least helped you fight those things.'

Eve felt like she'd slipped into some alternate universe, where the people looked the same, but were completely opposite inside. 'What are you talking about? I didn't take the sword.' She turned to Jess. 'And I didn't do anything to your dress. And I didn't hurt Peter on purpose. I'd never hurt him or any of you. How can you not know that?'

'I found your earring caught on the edge of my

bedspread,' Luke said. 'Right where it would be if it came off while you were grabbing the sword from under my bed.'

He turned to Jess. 'What time did the kung-fu class end?'

'We didn't end up going,' Jess answered.

'So you had plenty of time to go into my room while I was out jogging,' Luke accused. 'You weren't very careful, Eve. You forgot to put the blind back up, besides leaving your earring.'

He sounded so sure, like it was the only logical explanation. Jess, of course, didn't jump in to defend her. Alanna didn't comment, just watched from a metre or so away. But she was staring at Eve the same way Luke and Jess were – as if Eve was . . . God, it was like they thought she was evil.

Eve had to get away from those eyes. She turned and ran, almost falling as her foot slipped on a piece of vulture skin. She shoved her way through the double doors that led out to the playing fields, and kept on running.

I should check the portal, she thought. *That has to be where those disgusting things came from.*

But she didn't turn in the direction that would take her to the Medway mansion where the portal was.

Instead, she ran towards the station. She needed to get away, far away, out of this town, now that there was no barrier to keep her in. If everyone thought she was so horrible, they could take care of Deepdene by themselves.

'Everybody was in such a panic, they just ran straight out. I don't think anyone saw Eve use her juice,' Luke told Jess. They lingered in the quad, even though the first bell was about to ring. Alanna had taken off, and the school had sent a clean-up crew in to deal with the gym.

'Except Peter, but he's seen it before.' Jess couldn't stop thinking of the expression on her brother's face. Shocked and almost lifeless. She'd had her mom come and pick him up, making up a story about how he'd fallen and hit his head on one of the benches. She figured a concussion would explain how out of it Peter was. 'I don't know if he's going to get over it this time,' she added.

'I know how he feels,' Luke said.

He sounded as shocked and lifeless as Peter had looked. Jess probably did too. She could hardly think because nothing made sense any more. 'Maybe I should have told my mom I got a concussion too,' she said. 'I don't know if I can function enough to get through the day. Eve . . . Eve's been my best friend since practically for ever. I just don't . . .' A salty lump formed in her throat and she could hardly choke out another word. 'I feel like she's gone.'

'Did you notice . . .' Luke hesitated.

Jess swallowed hard. 'What?' she prompted. She needed to talk. She needed help understanding.

'Eve was especially upset right before those demon birds crashed through the window,' he said.

Jess nodded. 'Her face was all flushed and her fingers were twitching the way they do when her power is gearing up. For a second I thought she was going to shoot out some lightning, the way she did in my room.'

'Yeah, that's what I'm talking about. It seems like she's having a harder and harder time controlling herself. Her power. When she gets angry . . .'

'*Kapow*,' Jess said softly.

Luke leaned towards her, and when he spoke, his voice was hardly more than a whisper. 'Alanna thinks maybe the demon part of Eve is getting stronger: that's that why she's changed so much and why she keeps losing control. The timing of those birds really bothers me. It's like they showed up right when she was so upset that she could hardly keep it together.' He shoved his fingers through his hair. 'I feel like I shouldn't be saying that about her. Even after everything she's done. She stole the sword, Jess! And ruined your dress.'

Jess nodded. 'She's changed. So, so much.' She hesitated, then continued. 'Do you think maybe she made them come here, those hideous birds? Like Peter said, maybe she draws demons. Or, God, could she have called them with her power?' Jess brought one of her fingers to her lips. She'd broken herself of nail-biting in the seventh grade. But now she really, really wanted to.

'I'm thinking all kinds of bad things,' Luke admitted. 'I don't want to, but, well, you saw her that day in the forest. It's not a very big leap to go from that kind of destruction to calling up demons, is it?'

'But she fought against them,' Jess reminded him. 'They were attacking her. You saw the blood on her.'

'Maybe the demon part called the other demons up, but then the Eve part managed to take control and fight them.' Luke looked down at Eve's earring in his hand. He'd been holding it the whole time they'd been talking, but it seemed like he'd forgotten what it was until that moment. 'That demon the two of you fought, the slimy one? How was Eve feeling before it showed up?'

Jess thought back. 'She was really upset when we first got to my house. She thought both of us were against her. That we were siding with the Order about the force field.'

'The force field.' Luke shook his head. 'You know, Eve was right about that. They did put it up to control her. They wanted to observe her, and they sent Alanna here to check the situation out and let them know if Eve was a threat.'

'A threat?' Even after what had happened, it was almost impossible for Jess to think of her best friend that way.

'That's what she said,' Luke answered. 'What were you going to say about that other demon? Was Eve upset just before it appeared?'

'She was a lot more upset when she first got to my house. We watched a movie, and had some chocolate, and when she left, I thought she was feeling a lot better.' It had been such an Eve-and-Jess afternoon, after all. Nice. Normal. 'Then we fought the demon together, and she seemed totally on. It was even fun.'

'That's been bugging me too. How Eve finds

fighting fun. It's like she loves the violence in a way she didn't before,' Luke said.

'I had fun kicking that goopy thing's ass. I really did,' Jess said softly.

'You didn't steal from one of your friends. You didn't destroy something one of your friends loved,' Luke reminded her.

The dress. Her beautiful dress. Just thinking about it made Jess feel like crying. Thinking about Eve ripping it up made her feel even worse.

'What about the first Deepdene Witch?' Jess felt a surge of hope. 'She didn't go bad, at least nothing we've found out has said so. It seemed like she was helping people her whole life. And she had demon blood too.'

Luke scrubbed his forehead with his fingers. 'Maybe she was stronger than Eve. Maybe she was able to push the demon side down.' The first bell rang. 'I guess we have to go in. Be normal.'

Jess didn't know if she could. Not when she didn't know where Eve was. Or who she was.

Chapter Eleven

At least I got a new blouse out of the stinking heap of badness that's been my day so far. The thought didn't cheer Eve up the tiniest bit, even though the blouse was gorgeous, silk crepe with a vibe that was part military and part boho. Still, at least now she didn't have to walk around Manhattan in a shirt that had holes and rips and blood stains from the pecking and scratching of those hideous birds.

She hadn't exactly planned to go to the city. She'd run to the station, just wanting to get away, away, away. She'd gotten on the first train, and went into some kind of mental brown-out, not really thinking, rocking with the motion, staring out of the window without really seeing anything. Every train heading west ended in Manhattan, so when the ticket-collector had come round, she'd given that as her destination and paid.

It had been a good choice. There were so many people on the sidewalks, so many cars on the streets, so many sounds and smells and sights that Eve felt like a little speck of a thing, completely anonymous. Now that she'd gotten out of her bird-ravaged clothes, nobody even glanced at her. Nobody particularly cared about her. Which meant nobody hated her the way Luke and Jess did.

God, Luke and Jess *hated* her. Eve still hadn't quite figured out how that had happened. Sure, she'd had fights with both of them, but a fight was just a fight. Usually after you fought with your friends, you both said sorry and everything went back to normal. But instead, Jess started accusing her of shredding the prom dress and Luke accused her of stealing the sword, and both of them were acting like Eve had suddenly turned evil or something. Even though she'd saved the town – or at least part of it – once again. She'd saved most of the prom decorations too, thank you very much.

Eve stepped out of Bloomingdale's and started up Third Avenue. She couldn't stop herself from pausing in front of one of the store's huge window displays. There was a dress that would be perfect for Jess to wear to the prom. It was almost completely the opposite of the Dolce & Gabbana gown, which was a good thing. Jess didn't want to wear anything that would remind her of the ruined dress. And this dress wouldn't.

For starters, this dress was short, very short. And it didn't have a romantic feel, it was full-out sexy: silver, with a geometric pattern that looked like it could have come out of a cool sci-fi movie. The only thing it had in common with the other gown was that they were both complete show-stoppers. And that the pink crystal pendant would go great with both. It would really pop against the silver.

Should I go back in and put it on hold for her? The thought was automatic. It took a few seconds for Eve to remember that Jess would probably never even speak to her again. And Eve wouldn't want to talk to her anyway, not after the things that Jess had said in the gym.

Eve started walking again, picking up her pace to match the flow of the crowd. On 60th Street, she took a right. A frozen hot chocolate probably wouldn't make her feel any better than the new blouse did, but she always went to Serendipity when she was in Manhattan – she had since she was a little girl. And most of those times Jess had been with her.

It was totally touristy, but they loved it.

She really had to stop thinking about Jess. It hurt too much. She didn't want to think about Luke either. Not unless she wanted to end up crying on the streets of New York. *I don't want to end up crying in Serendipity either*, she told herself as she reached the restaurant's black awning. She managed to ask for a table for one in a voice that didn't tremble even a little. So far, so good.

Eve ordered lunch first, even though she wasn't hungry. But she needed a place to sit for a while and . . . and she didn't even know what. Calm down? Try to glue herself back together? What were you supposed to do when your whole world turned upside down?

To occupy herself while she waited for her food, she re-read the familiar menu. She wondered what Luke would have to say about the Golden Opulence Sundae, the most expensive sundae in the world. It cost a thousand dollars and had ingredients from all over the globe. Luke would probably—

Eve suddenly felt like she was breathing in little shards of glass. Why had she let her brain go there? The image of Luke's face twisted in anger as he yelled at her filled her mind. Thinking about him was as bad as thinking about Jess. She wondered how long it would keep hurting. She wondered if she'd ever actually be able to stop thinking of one or the other of them every few minutes.

It definitely hadn't happened by the time she finished her food and started on her frozen hot chocolate. Hot chocolate reminded her of Jess and Luke. They both knew—

'Eve! I knew you'd be here. When I couldn't find you anywhere in Deepdene, I knew it!'

It was Jess! Jess was flying across the room towards her. And she was smiling. Smiling, but with tears running down her face at the same time.

Eve stood up so fast that she almost knocked over the wrought-iron chair. 'What are you doing here?' she exclaimed.

Jess hugged her hard. 'I came to tell you I'm sorry. I've been the hugest idiot.'

'I'm sorry too!' Eve realized she'd also started crying.

'You don't have anything to be sorry for,' Jess protested.

'Yeah, I do.' They both sat down at Eve's table, and Eve wiped her eyes with a napkin. 'I'm sorry I got so mad at you and Luke when you guys said I shouldn't take the force field down without knowing what was going on. I just got stuck on the fact that they'd put it up in the first place. And, also, I *have* been jealous of you. Just a little,' she added quickly. 'I've been having panglets of jealousy. But it's not because you're going to the prom. It's just because I always thought we'd have the whole prom experience together.'

Jess teared up all over again. 'Oh. I'm an idiot. How could I not realize that? We've been talking about double-dating to the prom since we were five.'

'But I'm also so happy for you,' Eve added. 'And I think I found you a dress you'll love as much as the first one!'

'Really? Yay!' Jess exclaimed. 'And if you'd been going to the prom and I wasn't, I'd definitely have had panglets too.' She grabbed a napkin and dabbed at her tear-streaked face. 'Nice blouse . . . !'

'I still can hardly believe you're here,' Eve said after Jess had gotten set up with a frozen hot chocolate of her own. 'You were so mad when I left. What changed your mind?'

'When you ran off, I couldn't shake my feeling that . . . well, that I just didn't understand what was going on. And I got worried about you,' Jess explained.

'So then I realized that if I *really* thought you were a demon, I wouldn't be worried at all. I'd be glad that you left.'

'Hold on. You thought I was a demon?' Eve cried.

'Not completely a demon. Just maybe that the demon part of you was getting stronger than the *you* part of you.'

Eve stared at her, shocked. She didn't know what to say. She felt like she'd been hollowed out. Her best friend thought she was turning into a demon?

Jess put her hand on Eve's arm. 'That day in the woods, you were pretty scary,' she said softly. 'And then when Peter said you were in our house right before my dress was slashed . . .'

'But I wasn't there. I wasn't,' Eve insisted. 'I have no idea what Peter was talking about.'

'I believe you. I promise,' Jess told her. 'Like I said, I knew I wouldn't be feeling so worried about you if I really thought you were going all demony. And if you weren't going all demony, then, of course, you wouldn't rip up my dress. And you'd never hurt Peter. How could I have thought that? You're the one who saved Peter's life when Amunnic snatched him. You've saved lots of people, Eve.'

'Everything's so confusing.' Eve rubbed her

temples, hoping that would make her think more clearly. 'Why did Peter say I was at your house when I wasn't? And why did Luke accuse me of stealing the sword? Why would I steal his sword? I don't need it to fight demons, I have my zap.'

'I don't know about Peter. Maybe he got the day wrong. Or even the person wrong. He's been really out of it lately. Not all the time, but some of the time when I talk to him it's like he isn't even there. Kind of like that day when he was spaced out in front of the TV,' Jess answered. 'And as for Luke . . . you might have Alanna to thank for his weirdness.'

'Alanna? Why Alanna?' Eve had never liked the girl, but she hadn't done anything too awful during this visit. In fact, she'd been sort of decent.

'This morning after you . . . took off, Luke told me the Order sent Alanna to Deepdene to evaluate you. And you were right! They put up the force field so they could keep you contained while they observed to see what effect the demon blood had. I guess after you took the force field down, they were worried that you might be . . .' – Jess hesitated, then rushed on – 'a threat. And Alanna said that to Luke. She told him she thought your demon side might be taking control of you. I guess when he saw your earring and the sword was gone, he was primed to think bad things.'

Eve shook her head. 'I guess that explains why Alanna was so much nicer this time. She probably figured it would be easier to *evaluate* me if she acted like she was on my side.' She noticed that her frozen hot chocolate was becoming unfrozen, but she couldn't eat it. All this new info was making her dizzy. Luke thought she was going demon? How could he believe something like that if he cared about her at all?

Answer: he couldn't. He couldn't care about her. She was just some girl to him. A plaything for the player. She had to be. And she – she almost loved him. Or maybe she completely loved him.

Jess thought you were evil too, for a while, she reminded herself. *And setting the woods on fire isn't exactly normal girl behaviour*. It didn't make her feel any better about Luke.

'Alanna's a sneaky witch. No, that makes it sound like witches are bad, and you're a witch who's good. Alanna's a sneaky sneak. I bet she loved making Luke think something could be wrong with you,' Jess said.

'Well, it explains a lot,' Eve agreed. 'I'm less confuzzled.' She used the word she and Jess had come up with for a combination of confused and frazzled.

'I'm still confuzzled about the dress situation,' Jess

admitted. She nibbled on the chocolate stick from her dessert. 'Now that I'm sane again, I know you didn't do it. Can you believe I thought you would hurt a Dolce & Gabbana gown?'

'No. I can't believe that,' Eve said with a smile.

'But then who did?'

'I guess we're back to Simon,' Eve said slowly, trying to think it through. 'Even though he really sounded like he was telling the truth when Seth asked him about it.'

Jess snorted. 'We have to remember that Seth was about to punch Simon's face in. Maybe that gave him the motivation to lie really well. Although I thought he was telling the truth too. Especially when Seth was gone and he was talking just to us.' She spooned up a bite of her frozen hot chocolate, but didn't eat it. She stared around the restaurant, frowning.

'What?' Eve asked.

'I keep feeling like someone's watching me,' Jess explained. She licked the chocolate off her spoon, but she didn't seem to be tasting the yumminess. 'God, maybe Simon is still in stalker mode.'

'Well, Simon's no match for the two of us,' Eve assured her, trying to sound more like her old self. She glanced around the room too, but didn't see anything unusual. Except for the unusually hot guy – well, hot *man*: he was probably in his late twenties – who'd just walked in. 'Hel-lo,' she murmured, giving Jess a little chin-jerk so she'd look over and see him – him with his black hair, and eyes that were so dark there was almost no colour difference between pupil and iris.

'Wows,' Jess whispered back. Her eyes widened. 'Eve, he's coming right towards us.'

Eve tried to take another look without being obvious about it. But he caught her at it and held her gaze. He spoke into a small mic clipped to his lapel – the kind cops wore – as he strode over to them, his expression grim.

'Come with me.' He grabbed Eve's arm and pulled her to her feet.

'What? Where?' Eve exclaimed as he urged her to the door. Her heart skittered in her chest.

'Who are you? You can't just drag her out of here!' Jess exclaimed. When the man didn't stop marching Eve to the door, Jess pulled out her iPhone. 'You don't tell me, I'm calling the cops.'

The man snatched Jess's phone without releasing his grip on Eve. 'This doesn't concern you.' Eve noticed he had a slight Spanish accent. She tried to memorize everything about him. He wasn't going to get away with this.

'Of course it does! She's my best friend!' Jess cried.

They didn't need the cops. Or a phone. All they needed was a loud scream. Eve opened her mouth.

'You don't want to do that,' the man told her. 'I'm with the Order. We're connected all over this city. All over the world.'

Eve's mouth snapped shut. She exchanged a panicked glance with Jess. The Order? She was being kidnapped by the Order. Had Alanna sent in her report? What were they going to do to her?

She imagined herself locked in a cell for the rest of her life. If they even let her live. The thought turned her knees to water. If the man didn't have her arm, she wasn't sure she'd be able to stand.

'Is everything all right, girls?' the waitress called as they reached the door.

'Fine,' Eve told her, forcing a smile. She quickly fished inside her purse and threw some money down on the counter to pay for the food and frozen hot chocolates. The waitress couldn't help. If Eve tried to involve her, she might end up getting hurt.

'We're OK,' Jess added as the three of them hurried out of the café.

'In,' the man ordered, opening the back door of a black sedan that was parked in front of the restaurant.

Eve's brain whirled as she tried to decide what to do. She couldn't use her power on him. He was human. And the Order would be able to find her wherever she went. Payne had sensed her when he was in Deepdene, and this man had found her among all the people in Manhattan.

'You know what? There are some things I'd like to talk to the Order about too.' Like trapping her in her own town. Like one of their members turning her boyfriend against her. She slid into the car, chin high. She hoped he believed the brave front she was putting up. Jess clambered in beside her.

'Not you,' the man said.

'Where she goes, I go,' Jess said. 'And I don't care who you are. If I start screaming about my best friend being abducted, somebody will listen.'

He didn't answer. Just shut the car door, then got in the front seat. He started the engine and locked the doors centrally from the dashboard.

'Thanks, Jess. Thank you so much.' Eve didn't want her friend to be in danger, but it felt good, so, so good, not to be in this car all alone.

'Like I was going to let you have this big adventure

207

all by yourself.' Jess wasn't bad at putting up a front either.

As the car pulled away from the kerb, Eve noticed that there were no locks on the back doors. There was no way to get out. She began shivering uncontrollably. Jess grabbed her hand, and her friend's fingers were cold and clammy. 'What are we going to do?' Jess whispered.

'I don't know.' Eve hated to say the words. They filled her with hopelessness and despair. But there was no other way to answer Jess.

In what felt like seconds, although it was probably a ten-block ride, the car glided over to the kerb and stopped.

The man, who hadn't said a word the whole ride, climbed out and opened the back door. He gestured for them to get out. Why had Eve thought he was hot? Now he just looked scary. What did he need all those muscles for anyway?

When she stepped out of the car, Eve was surprised at how ordinary the block looked. A row of town-houses on one side of the street, a large apartment building and more townhouses on the other. The only strange thing was that the block was quiet, way too quiet for Manhattan.

Eve didn't have much time to think about it. The man whisked her and Jess up the steps of the nearest townhouse. It looked just like the others on the block, but Eve was willing to bet that it didn't take a retina scan to get into *those* buildings. Once the man's scan was approved, the lock on the door clicked open.

'Inside,' he said.

'Impressive vocabulary on you,' Jess commented.

At least neither of us is letting this Order goon see how afraid we really are, Eve thought as she stepped into the foyer. She couldn't see much more than the large marble staircase rising in front of them and the rug that lay in front of that.

A creepy rug. Around the border were little faces; some seemed almost human, some not so much.

'Upstairs,' the man told them. He let her and Jess go up the polished marble steps ahead of him.

'Now down there,' he instructed when they reached the top, pointing to the last doorway on the left. The hall was lined with paintings.

'I think that's an original Hieronymus Bosch,' Jess whispered, nodding towards one that showed an old man surrounded by fantastical and grotesque creatures. She'd gone to a ton of museums on a European vacation with her parents.

'Impressive eye for art,' the man said. Was he attempting a sense of humour now? Didn't he know there was nothing funny about being abducted?

When they reached the last doorway, the man reached over Eve's shoulder and knocked. There was another retina scanner outside, but the door was opened from within.

'Callum!' Eve exclaimed. She didn't know why she was surprised to see him. She'd known he was high up in the Order. But somehow she just hadn't thought about the fact that he must have been the one who gave instructions to haul her in. She'd seen the man talking into his mic as soon as he'd spotted her, but she hadn't stopped to think who he was communicating with.

'Come in, Eve, Jess. Come sit down. Can we get you something to drink?' Callum asked.

'Can you get us something to drink?' Eve repeated, outraged. 'You had this man kidnap me and now you're acting like we're all friends?'

Callum raised an eyebrow. 'I'm sorry if Carlos was . . . abrupt,' he said, his voice low and calm. 'It's just that when he discovered your presence in the city, I felt I needed to see you immediately. Please, sit. I have a few questions.'

They both sat down on the overstuffed flowered sofa in front of Callum's big desk. The room had a strange mix of elements. The sofa, desk, the row of bookshelves, the huge dictionary on one stand, and the globe on another all looked old-fashioned. But the ultra-thin laptop on the desk was super high-tech, and there were small security cameras mounted in two corners of the ceiling.

Besides the old and the cutting edge were a bunch of things that were just . . . weird. Over on the bookshelf was what looked like a thigh bone with dozens of tiny dragons carved into it. On the desk, Callum was using a chunk of rock as a paperweight. Brownish red streaks crisscrossed it and Eve was pretty sure those streaks were blood. Amulets on chains and cords hung down over all three of the room's windows.

'How have you been, Eve?' Callum asked as he sat in an armchair to the right of the sofa. Carlos – that was the man's name, Carlos – remained standing, positioning himself across from Callum.

'I've been completely pissed off, as you've probably heard. You trapped me in Deepdene – or tried to.'

Callum leaned forward, clasping his hands together. 'We did. We weren't sure whether or not you were dangerous,' he said simply. 'Which leads me to this question – *how* are you here? How were you able to leave? Your arrival in the city triggered an alert here; Carlos was expecting to bring in a demon. He didn't realize until he was at the restaurant that what we had sensed as demon presence was actually the Deepdene Witch.'

'I have a question first. Where are we?' Eve demanded.

'This is the headquarters of the New York branch of the Order,' Callum answered. 'We have branches all over the world.' His tone continued to be genial. 'I've answered your question. Now would you please tell me how you left Deepdene with the barrier in place?'

'You underestimated how strong my power is,' Eve told him. 'I blasted your barrier down. Why are you pretending you don't know that?'

His eyes widened. 'Your power broke down the protective barrier?' He sounded surprised. Eve didn't get it.

'Yes, and you already know that!' she cried, frustrated. 'Alanna gave you a report. I know you sent her to Deepdene to evaluate me, to decide if I'm a *threat*.'

Carlos cursed under his breath. An expression of alarm briefly crossed Callum's face.

Eve glanced back and forth between Carlos and Callum. 'What's going on?'

'I didn't send Alanna to Deepdene,' Callum replied. 'I didn't even know where she was. As far as I know, she's been missing since Sunday night. She hasn't answered any of our calls or texts. We've all been very worried about her.'

'What? Well, I saw her this morning,' Eve told him. 'She seemed just great. She was busy basically destroying my life.'

'She's been saying horrible things to Luke,' Jess burst in. 'Trying to make him believe Eve is evil.'

Callum's brow furrowed. 'I don't understand. I thought perhaps she had been taken by a demon or even killed. There was no other reason I could imagine for her breaking contact with us.'

'What else can you tell us about her actions?' Carlos asked.

'Luke got in touch with her just after I blasted through the barrier. He also told her about these dead animals around the border of the town. Alanna supposedly came to town to help. She said she didn't approve of the Order putting up the barrier at all.'

'Let's go back to the barrier for a moment. I'm disturbed,' Callum said, the lines around his mouth growing deeper. 'Eve, the magic we used to seal Deepdene is ancient and extremely powerful. There's no way you, even with your tremendous power, could have broken it. There has to be another explanation.'

'Well, here I am,' Eve told him, flinging her arms wide. 'I got out.'

'Callum, Alanna knows the ritual to destroy the barrier,' Carlos commented, his voice tight with anger. 'She could have performed it. The dead animals would have been necessary for that.'

'What you're suggesting is that Alanna could have betrayed us. That is a serious accusation,' Callum said.

'But it fits what we're hearing,' Carlos went on.

Callum shook his head. 'Although,' he continued, frowning, 'Alanna has always been the one cautioning us to be wary of the Deepdene Witch. I can't believe she thought we were wrong to try to contain . . .' His words trailed off.

Eve decided to help him out. 'To contain me. To keep me in a prison.'

'Only until we were certain you weren't dangerous,' Callum told her. 'That's the purpose of the Order. To keep humanity safe from demons.'

'But Eve isn't a demon!' Jess exclaimed.

'A part of her is.' Callum pressed his fingers to his temples. 'I'm trying to understand why Alanna would do this.'

'Callum, no matter what her reason, she's gone rogue. I know she was Payne's protégé, but it's clear that she's broken with us,' Carlos said, his voice raised. 'She knows so much, so many of our secrets. We must—'

'Something's messed up,' Eve exclaimed.

'A bunch of somethings,' corrected Jess.

'I mean about the timing. They said Alanna has been missing since Sunday night, but I took the barrier down on Sunday afternoon. Or I thought I did,' Eve explained.

'Which doesn't make sense. How could Alanna do a ritual to take down the barrier when she wasn't in Deepdene?' Jess jumped in. 'She would have had to be there to kill the animals. Was she in town for a while without us knowing?'

'And the dead animals had already been in the woods for a few days before the barrier came down,' Eve said. She turned to Callum. 'Are you sure I couldn't be strong enough to destroy it? Or what about another demon?'

215

'There was another demon in town on Sunday! A big squishy one!' Jess exclaimed. 'Eve and I killed it, but maybe before that it wrecked the barrier.'

'You fought a demon on Sunday?' Carlos demanded. 'What kind was it?'

'I don't really know demons by category,' Eve told him. Luke was trying to get together that database, but they'd only had experience of four different kinds of demons so far.

'It was sort of warm Jell-O-ish,' Jess volunteered. 'And it turned into a puddle of goo when we killed it.'

'It was gigantic, but it seemed like it was only partly formed,' Eve added.

'No matter what type of demon it was, it couldn't destroy the barrier,' Callum said. 'The ritual to remove it is one of our most closely guarded secrets. Alanna only knew it because she was hand-picked by Willem, and he was one of our most trusted members.'

'You were right to trust him,' Jess said. 'He died fighting demons. He probably saved my life. Eve and Luke's too.'

Eve realized things were more serious than she had thought. 'You should know that Willem's sword is missing – the sword he gave to Luke,' she said. 'Someone took it from Luke's room.'

216

'Another Alanna connection.' Callum let out a deep sigh, and he looked older than he had when Eve and Jess had first come into his office. 'Alanna is one of only three people who know Luke has the sword. I would have kept the information between Carlos and myself; he's my second in command here in New York. But Alanna came with me to reclaim Willem's body, and so she found out what had happened to the sword.' He shook his head, his face distressed. 'I just have no idea why she would have done all this.'

He stood up suddenly. 'We have to get to Deepdene. We have to find Alanna immediately.' He looked over at Carlos. 'I want to bring an armed squad.'

Chapter Twelve

Luke felt as if the school day had lasted about a year and a half. He hadn't been able to stop thinking about Eve. If the demon part of her had somehow called those vulture demons to it, then she could be in danger. Everyone in Deepdene could be in danger.

And Jess . . . Where *was* she? As far as he could figure, she'd taken off right after they had their conversation about Eve. He hadn't seen her at school all day. Was she looking for Eve? Because that could go very badly.

He turned up the walkway to the rectory, trying to decide what to do. Maybe he should try to track down Eve, but truthfully, he wasn't sure what he'd do if he found her. She was so powerful, and her power wasn't really under her control any more.

Maybe it would be better to get in touch with Alanna and strategize. But Alanna was so convinced that the demon part of Eve was taking her over, and he hadn't made up his mind yet whether he believed that or not.

I have to go after Eve myself, he decided as he entered the house. He'd drop off his backpack upstairs and check his email. Maybe she'd tried to get in touch. He doubted it, but it couldn't hurt to check.

Luke trotted up the stairs, then hurried into his room. His eyes widened and he let his backpack fall to the floor. Alanna was waiting on his bed, stretched out on her side with a little smirk on her lips.

'Uh, I'd say make yourself at home, but clearly you already did,' Luke said, trying to hide his shock. She'd just made her way into his house. How ballsy was that? 'Has something else happened? Did Eve—'

Alanna cut him off, her voice sharp. 'I'm not here to talk about your girlfriend problems.'

Luke took a couple of steps closer to her. 'Why are you here then?'

'I realized that I hadn't said thank you for my beautiful present.' She reached behind her, and picked up the sword from the bed. 'I love it.'

'*You* stole the sword?' Luke demanded.

'Of course I did,' Alanna purred.

Luke's mind spun. It had been Alanna, and he'd accused Eve. *Eve.* 'What were you—'

Before he could finish the question, something hard slammed into the back of his head. As he fell to his knees, the world around him went black.

'We said that the timing didn't work for Alanna to be the one who destroyed the barrier,' Carlos said. 'I keep going back to that. The evidence all points to her, but the pieces don't fit.'

Eve, Jess, Callum and Carlos were driving towards Deepdene in one of the Order's limousines. A van with a squad of four Order warriors followed.

'She could have had assistance from someone inside Deepdene. The ritual is a deep secret, but anyone who has the knowledge can perform it. It doesn't take special powers,' Callum replied. 'If she has found someone to help, the person is probably a loner, someone who doesn't attract a lot of attention. Quite possibly this person may be emotionally unstable, or might have been acting oddly lately. That would make it easier for Alanna to influence them,' Callum explained. 'Eve, Jess, is there anyone you can think of who fits that description?'

Eve and Jess exchanged a look. 'Simon,' they said at the same time.

'He's this guy at our school, and he's so like what

you said,' Jess told Callum. 'He doesn't have any friends, really. He's always off by himself in the library. And he got kind of obsessed with me. He was stalking me. So that's a yes on the emotionally unstable.'

'We caught him hanging around Jess's house,' Eve added. 'Then we found a dead cat almost right where he'd been. The cat had its throat sliced open, just like the dead animals Luke found around the border.'

Jess wrapped her arms tightly around herself. 'Do you think he'd been about to bring Pumpkin – that's the cat – to the border to work the ritual?'

At the word 'ritual' a thought hit Eve with the power of a punch. 'The ritual! It reversed a barrier to keep demons out. Could it have taken down the block I put over the portal too? Because that demon we fought had to come from somewhere.'

'And the demon birds!' Jess added.

'It's possible the ritual could have removed the protection that keeps demons from coming through the portal, yes. That protection and our barrier serve almost identical purposes,' Callum answered.

'What did you mean about demon birds?' Carlos asked.

'They attacked at school this morning. They were

like vultures, only supernatural. They smashed into the gym,' Eve said.

'This is all looking extremely dangerous.' Callum's skin had taken on a grey cast. 'A demon-killing sword stolen. The barrier down. The portal open. Demons invading. And Alanna seemingly having deserted the Order.'

Eve gasped in horror.

'What's wrong, Evie?' Jess cried.

'Luke! He doesn't know any of this. He has no idea what's going on.' Luke still thought Alanna was with the Order. He wouldn't have any reason to believe he had to protect himself against her. 'I've got to warn him.' She yanked her phone out of her bag and hit Luke's speed dial number.

The phone rang once . . . twice . . . three times, and she held her breath the whole time.

'Hello, Eve.'

Eve drew in a sharp breath. It felt like a layer of ice was forming inside her. That wasn't Luke's voice.

'Alanna!' she exclaimed, so everyone in the limo would know who she was talking to. 'You better not hurt my boyfriend. You know what I can do to you.' She put on the speaker so they could all hear.

Carlos pointed to himself, then Callum, and shook

his head. Eve got it. He didn't want her to let it slip that she was with a team from the Order. She nodded.

'Are you sure he's still your boyfriend? There's gossip going around that he hasn't been too happy with you lately. That was quite a scene the two of you made in the gym this morning,' Alanna answered, her voice soft and silky. Eve felt her power flare. She used all her will to shove it down. She wasn't wasting even a few sparks. She wanted all her fire when she faced Alanna.

'Thanks to you. You set me up. You made Luke think I was going demon and that I stole the sword. You planted my earring in his room,' Eve accused her.

'Me?' Alanna cried, all innocence. 'Well, maybe. That sounds like something I might do,' she added.

'Let me talk to Luke,' Eve demanded.

'You want him, you'll have to come get him,' Alanna taunted her.

'Just tell me where,' Eve said.

'The portal. As soon as it's dark.' Alanna hung up before Eve could get another word in.

'We can get there by dark, right?' she demanded.

'It'll be close,' Carlos replied. By car it took about two and a half hours to travel from the city to Deepdene. 'But I'll make sure we do.' He pressed a button, and the glass barrier between them and the driver slid down. 'Go as fast as you safely can,' Carlos instructed him. 'Ignore the speed limit.' He slid the glass back up.

'Jess, she has Luke,' Eve said miserably. The thought was pounding through her brain over and over. *She has Luke. She has Luke. She has Luke.*

'I know, sweetie,' Jess answered. 'But we're on our way to save him. We're going to save him.'

It was so good to have Jess here. Eve didn't know how she'd get through this without her. And their whole friendship had almost been destroyed by Alanna.

Callum shook his head. 'She had us all fooled. To me, she always seemed completely devoted to the Order,' he said. It sounded as if he were talking more to himself than to the rest of them. 'She was almost always monitoring possible trouble areas or researching.'

'She definitely spent a lot of time monitoring me,' Eve muttered. 'And I even helped! She asked me all about my powers, and I just answered like it was nothing.'

'We can handle Alanna,' Jess said firmly.

But she has Luke. The thought continued to loop. *She has Luke. She has Luke. She has Luke.*

'You're going to kick her ass, Evie,' Jess continued. 'And I'm going to help.'

Eve held on to that promise all the way to Deepdene. 'Don't get too close to the Medway mansion,' she told Callum as they drove into town. 'I don't think we should give away the fact that I have backup from the Order. Not until I see what the situation is.'

'Something's not right,' Jess said, staring out the window. 'I can't figure out what.'

Eve leaned towards the window too. 'The power's out,' she breathed. 'You don't notice right away, because there's still a tiny bit of sunlight. But look, there's no light on in any of the houses, and the streetlights should be on by now.'

'Alanna,' Jess said.

Eve nodded. 'She knows I can get power from electricity. She did this.' She pulled in a deep breath. 'Doesn't matter. I have juice. But it's not like I plan on using it. Alanna's still a human. She just better not try to hurt Luke. She does that, I'll use everything I have.'

'We're going to park round the corner,' Carlos said. 'The squad will be watching, and be able to get to you in seconds whenever you need them.' He radioed instructions back to the van.

Eve scrambled out of the car. Callum and Carlos started to get out behind her. 'No,' she told them. 'You're staying here too. This is my town. This is my responsibility. This is *my* fight.'

'You're going to let me help though, right?' Jess asked as she stepped out of the limo. 'I want to bring my kung-fu down on Alanna. I've never trusted her.'

'I don't think that's a good idea,' Callum said, peering out though the open door. 'Jess, you don't have any training.'

'She has training. On-the-job training,' Eve shot back. 'She's been with me for every demon fight. And she's going to be with me now.' She grabbed Jess's hand, and they ran down the dark street and round the corner.

Eve could see flames on the old Medway property. As she and Jess raced through the gate and across the wildly overgrown lawn, she realized that Alanna had placed torches on either side of the ancient stone portal.

When they reached the portal, Eve's eyes darted back and forth as she tried to take in everything at once. Alanna leaned against the stone arch, all casual, a little smile on her smug face.

And Luke! Luke lay on the ground, his hands and

feet bound with rope. But even worse than that was the figure who stood over him. Eve tried to see who – or what – it was, but a hood was drawn way down over the face. Could it be Simon? That was definitely the demon-hunting sword he held pressed against Luke's throat.

The portal was definitely open. The web of power that Eve had placed across it months ago had always given off a slight electric buzz. That sound was gone now. Was Alanna going to call something out of there that she'd have to fight? She'd probably learned some methods of summoning demons while she was with the Order.

'I've been waiting a long time for this,' Alanna said. 'And I've been looking forward to it.' She pushed herself away from the arch, but didn't move closer to Eve.

Jess touched Eve's arm, drawing her attention over to Luke. He kept looking back and forth from the portal to Alanna. He was trying to tell her something, but Eve wasn't sure what. Maybe that Alanna had opened the portal. She gave him a little nod then turned her full attention back to Alanna.

'What do you want?' Eve said. 'Just say it and let's get this over with.'

'Feisty,' Alanna commented. 'You've always been a

feisty little girl.' She took one step closer to Eve. 'Here's what I want. I want to kill you.'

'You'll have to go through me,' Jess told her.

'I thought you'd be way too mad at Eve for ruining your prom dress,' Alanna said. 'But if you want me to kill you too, I suppose I can manage it.'

'It was *you* who destroyed my dress!' Jess burst out, furious.

'And you stole the sword too!' Eve cried – the sword, which was now pressed against Luke's throat. Eve didn't allow herself to glance back over at him. She couldn't get distracted. Not now.

'I had a little help,' Alanna said. 'Sadly, I wasn't able to do everything by myself, much as I'd have loved to.'

Eve glanced at the hooded figure. It must be Simon. He must have been helping Alanna with everything, from killing the animals to destroying Jess's dress.

'Why would you do that?' Jess demanded. 'I know you don't like me, but that's what you spend your time doing? Mutilating dresses?'

Alanna said with a shrug, 'I thought it would be nice to force you and Miss Eve into a fight. That way, your friend wouldn't get any help from you or—' She jerked her head at Luke.

'Well, it didn't work,' Jess snapped.

228

'It almost did, admit it,' Alanna teased her. 'You thought your little friend was jealous enough to ruin your pretty dress.' She looked over at Eve. 'You should know that I had your boyfriend convinced you were dangerous and evil. It wasn't hard. That distrust was already in him.'

Luke gave a sound of protest through his gag. Alanna wagged her finger at him. 'Now, now. You know it's true. I saw it on your face. You believed that Eve called those vulture demons to her. You believed she stole your sword. You believed everything I wanted you to believe.' She winked at Eve. 'If that's not love, what is?

'So what do you think, Eve? I like the idea of battling you without your entourage. After all, my last fight with the Deepdene Witch was one-on-one.'

Alanna was getting crazier by the second. 'We've never fought,' Eve told her.

'Not you. Great-great-great-grandma.'

Eve's mind raced for a second, then understanding slammed through her. She stared in horror at Alanna. 'You're the girl. I mean, you're the *demon*. The demon the Deepdene Witch zapped hard enough to bury inside a human.'

'Ah, there you go. You figured it out. Finally. You're

feisty, but you aren't exactly quick, are you?' Alanna asked.

'A demon. Well, now a lot of things about you are making sense!' Jess exclaimed, awesome as always. Eve was going to make sure nothing bad happened to her.

'You want to fight me alone. Fine. Let's do it.' Eve met Alanna's gaze directly. 'Let Luke and Jess go. You said you didn't want them with me.'

'Oh, they're already here. I think they should be allowed to watch,' Alanna said. 'Not that it will take long. I've studied your fighting style, and you were nice enough to tell me some titbits I didn't know, like the way you can suck down electricity. Killing you won't be difficult. You've noticed I shut off the power in town.'

Jess started to rush at Alanna, but Eve caught her by the arm. Alanna laughed. 'I'm happy to use her as a warm-up before the main event.'

'No. You said it was me you wanted. Just me.' She kept her grip on Jess's arm.

'I did go to a lot of trouble for that,' Alanna mused, then gave another little shrug. 'She can fight or she can watch or she can run. It doesn't really matter.'

'Let Simon go too.'

'Simon? I almost laughed when I heard he was

the one you suspected. No, Simon's not my helper. Doesn't matter who it is. Time to dispose of him anyway. Possessing him takes too much strength.'

Eve gasped as Alanna reached towards Luke. She didn't touch him. Instead, she made a grabbing motion in the air, and the hooded figure slumped to the ground with a grunt, dropping the sword.

'No!' Jess cried, cringing as the sword clattered on the ground. The hood slipped off, revealing Peter's face, unconscious. Jess rushed over and dropped to her knees next to her little brother. 'How could you do this to him?' she cried.

'He was the perfect choice,' Alanna answered. 'Possessions are a little tricky, but I had an in, since your friend there had frightened Peter so badly back when she was fighting Amunnic. A few emails and phone calls about my fears for anyone around Eve, and he was nice and loosened up. It wasn't hard to take it from there.'

'Possession? You possessed Peter?' Jess shouted. Eve could see she was torn between staying at her brother's side and attacking the demon.

'Mmm-hmm. It was *so* convenient,' Alanna told Jess. 'Peter had no problem getting inside your house to destroy the dress, because he lived there. And it was easy to have him feed you the lies that made you doubt Eve more and more.'

A rush of nausea passed through Eve as she realized what had happened. 'You made him kill all those animals for the ritual too!' she cried.

'Oh, I had him do all kinds of things. The ritual was crucial, obviously. I've been waiting to fight you for so long, and when the Order put up the barrier it did create an additional . . . challenge. Just as it kept you in, it kept me out. I knew I needed someone inside the town to get rid of it for me. Peter summoned those vulture demons in the gym, too. When I heard about that slimy demon you fought, I realized the ritual had also knocked down the barrier over the portal. Those birds were a great way to make Luke trust you even less.'

Luke gave another grunt of protest. Alanna picked up the sword. 'Time for me to get my life back. I've been waiting a hundred years for the new Deepdene Witch to appear. That's why I joined the Order. I knew they would have the information I needed to find you and the details about what I would have to do to be free. And it turned out to be easy. Kill you. That's all I have to do.'

'Then why don't you stop talking and bring it on?'

Eve challenged. Out of the corner of her eye, she saw Jess rise to her feet. 'Stay with Peter. He needs you,' she called. 'Alanna wants this one-on-one, which is fine with me!'

More than fine. All Eve wanted was to take Alanna down.

Alanna raised the sword up, both hands wrapped around the hilt. Then she rushed at Eve, bringing the blade down, aiming for the top of her head.

Eve ducked, and threw out both hands, shooting lightning into Alanna's belly. Alanna screeched. As Eve spun to the right, Alanna followed her motion with the blade, making a thin, shallow cut on Eve's side.

Eve gasped in pain. It felt like the sword was carved from dry ice. It was so cold, it almost felt hot. Steam billowed from the cut as Eve backed up. She needed a little distance from Alanna. The range of Eve's power was a lot longer than the range of Alanna's sword.

Alanna shook her head, her hair going from smooth and sleek to snagged, coarse and greasy. 'That feels wonderful!' Her voice had changed too, deepened and roughened.

As Eve continued to back up, Alanna advanced, swinging the sword in wide, whistling arcs. Eve took aim at one of Alanna's shoulders. Alanna twisted her body and intercepted the lightning with the sword. Balls of fire bounced off the blade. One grazed Eve's cheek as it sped back.

She'd already been hit twice, and hadn't managed a successful attack on Alanna. 'You're doing half my fighting for me!' Alanna crowed in that horrible new voice of hers. Her mouth opened in a manic grin and Eve could see dozens of sharp little teeth. The demon was coming out! With each blow Alanna struck, she was regaining more of her demonic self.

Eve aimed her next blast low. She shoved her power out in a straight stream. It sizzled as it hit Alanna's kneecap. Eve kept blasting. Alanna howled with pain, but she managed to get the blade in the path of Eve's power. For a moment it was like a laser light show. A thin red line of fire hitting the sword, then being shot back at an angle.

Eve raised her hands, bringing the stream of power up. Alanna followed it with the sword, and her power continued to shoot back towards her.

Her hands! I have to go for her hands, Eve realized. If she could get Alanna to drop the sword, she could turn this round.

She did something she hoped Alanna wouldn't expect. She hurled herself at the demon. In a split second she was upon her, wrapping her hands round Alanna's. Eve was so close, Alanna couldn't get the space she needed to strike.

Alanna's skin went red as Eve sent her power right into the demon's hands. Eve could see the bones glowing white-hot. But Alanna didn't drop the sword. Eve needed more power. But Alanna had taken away every source.

Then suddenly Alanna stamped on Eve's instep. Startled, Eve stumbled back, losing her grip, and before she could recover, Alanna was on her, slashing, slashing. She got Eve on the thigh, and then on the calf of the other leg. Both wounds turned numb with cold, making it hard for her to keep her balance.

'I should have let you bring your friends to the fight,' Alanna called, her skin withering as she spoke, withering and taking on a sickly yellow-white tone. Her pupils widened until they blocked out the irises, and the whites of Alanna's eyes turned red. 'You obviously need backup.'

'I'm coming in!' Jess yelled.

'No!' Eve shouted. 'Stay with Peter.' Alanna was beating her despite her powers. Jess wouldn't stand a chance.

When Alanna slashed at her again with the sword,

Eve managed to leap over it. But when she landed, her numb legs wouldn't support her. She fell onto her back.

Alanna stepped up and put her foot on Eve's chest. She was almost fully transformed now, her back humped, talons where her perfectly manicured nails had been.

Eve glimpsed something behind Alanna. She couldn't see well from the ground, but she thought the Order squad was approaching.

'The things I'm going to do now that I'm rid of that weak body,' Alanna crowed, and as she spoke droplets of acid dripped from her mouth, landing on Eve and slowly beginning to burn through her clothes. 'I know the location of every known portal. I'm going to use the ritual to free every demon in existence. This world will finally be ours!'

A branch cracked, as if someone had stepped on it. Alanna jerked her head towards the sound, the pressure of her foot lessening. Eve rolled out from under it, breathing hard.

'Callum!' Alanna exclaimed, spotting the Order head. 'What a surprise! How does it feel knowing you had a demon right in the heart of the Order without ever realizing it? A demon who is going to destroy everything the Order has built.'

'You were deeply buried inside the girl,' Callum answered calmly. 'We never suspected you. Things will be different now that you've revealed yourself. You know many of the Order's secrets, but you have no idea of all we're capable of.'

As Callum spoke, Eve used both hands to shove herself upright. She swayed on her unsteady legs, catching sight of Jess, Peter and Luke, crowded together at the base of the portal.

Alanna had tried to take away the people she loved. She'd used Peter as a puppet, making him do horrible things, making him perform the hideous ritual that allowed her to enter Deepdene. She'd tried to make Luke and Jess hate Eve. *Hate her!* Eve was not going to let Alanna win, no matter how hurt she herself got in the process. Hot power exploded inside her, her love for her friends more of a power boost than any session at the power plant. It banished the coldness from her body.

With a shout of fury, Eve launched herself at Alanna. The demon was facing Callum, and that allowed Eve to grab her from behind. She locked her hands together, pulling Alanna back against her. The sword couldn't touch Eve now.

Her power erupted with a light so bright and white it blocked out everything else. It shot from her entire body. She could feel it flying from the ends of her hair, shooting from her belly, her head, her arms, her legs.

It felt like her body was dissolving into pure power. Like soon there'd be nothing left of her.

If it killed Alanna, it would be worth it.

Eve didn't hold back. She turned herself over to the power. The world went silent – white and silent.

Then, faintly, she heard Jess calling her name. Eve followed the sound back. It felt as if she was returning from another galaxy.

She managed to blink, then blink again. The blinding white blur that surrounded her faded. Eve stared around, drinking in the sight of Luke, and of Jess, cradling Peter in her arms, of the portal, Callum and Carlos, of the squad who had come to her rescue.

She didn't see Alanna anywhere. 'Where is she?'

Jess pointed to the ground. When Eve looked down, she saw the sword – the sword and some bloody shreds of flesh and tiny bits of bone.

'That was . . . astonishing,' Callum said, eyes wide.

'Yeah,' Eve agreed. All she felt at that moment was empty, as if she'd been hollowed out. Killing Alanna had almost killed her too.

'Well, we have a lot to discuss, but for now, let's get the portal closed up.' Callum waved over the other members of the Order. They all formed a line in front of the arch and began to chant.

'Eve!' Jess called again.

The sound of her voice pierced Eve's numbness. She hurried over to her friends. 'Is Peter OK?' she asked Jess.

Jess nodded, her eyes shiny with unshed tears. 'He's in and out, but he's OK.'

Eve turned to Luke. He'd managed to work the gag free and spit it out. 'I was wondering if my girlfriend could untie me,' he said, his voice husky. 'If she's through saving the town – again.'

'On it.' Eve went to retrieve the sword. Girlfriend. He'd called her his girlfriend. Girlfriend had to be the most wonderful word in the world – at least it was when Luke was saying it about her.

She returned to him and knelt down. 'By the way, it wasn't just the town this time. It was the world. Didn't you hear Alanna say she was going to release all the demons and take over the planet?' she asked as she carefully used the sword to cut Luke free.

'Are you OK?' he asked, running his fingers down

her cheek as soon as his hands were released. 'Saving the world. That's quite a job.'

'I think I'm OK,' Eve said. 'I had these numb spots from getting cut by the sword, but they feel all right now.' She felt her side, where the blade had sliced her. Her skin felt smooth and warm. 'What about you?'

'Well, physically I'm fine. But I feel pretty stupid. Alanna manipulated me so easily,' Luke replied. 'In addition to the world-saving, you think you could manage to forgive me?'

'Absolutely,' Eve told him. She balanced the sword across her open palms and held it out to him. 'This belongs to you.'

Luke's green eyes were solemn when he took the sword from her. 'I'll always be there, with this sword, whenever you need me,' he promised.

'Eve,' Callum called. Reluctantly she looked away from Luke. 'We've done what we can to seal the portal. We need you to finish it off. Do you think you have enough power left?'

That explosion of power had left her feeling somehow cleansed inside, scrubbed clean. But she could feel a spark in the centre of her ribcage. 'Let me try,' she answered.

She stepped in front of the arch, the members of

the Order moving back. She closed her eyes and focused on the spark. 'You can do this, Eve!' Luke called. And the spark brightened.

'Go, Evie!' Jess exclaimed. And the spark expanded into a ball about the size of Eve's fist. She thought about all the people she loved, and all the people who loved her, and the ball grew bigger, brighter and hotter.

She thought about all the people in the town, all of them needing her protection, and then she was ready. She opened her eyes and raised her arms in front of her. Waves of undulating golden light stretched from her fingers to the portal. Strands of light began to stretch back and forth across the opening, crisscrossing, forming a dense net of protection.

Eve smiled. She loved using her power this way, to heal and mend instead of fight. But she was ready to fight again, whenever Deepdene – or the earth – was in danger.

Epilogue

'I knew that dress would look awesome on you,' Eve told Jess. They stood in front of the full-length mirror in Jess's bedroom.

'I think I'll keep you on as my personal shopper,' Jess teased her. Eve had gotten up early the morning after she'd defeated Alanna and gone to Bloomingdale's as soon as it opened. She'd bought the silver-on-silver dress, figuring she could return it if Jess didn't like it. Not that she really thought that was possible. And she had been right. Jess and the dress? Love-match.

'I feel like some kind of kickass princess from another planet. Maybe Planet Fashion.' Jess turned from side to side, admiring the fit of her short, sexy dress.

'That's how I always think of you,' Eve joked back.

Jess turned to Eve and adjusted the jewelled clip

that held a section of Eve's curly hair away from her face. The clip matched the jewelled scoop neck on Eve's deep blue dress. 'You look beautiful,' Jess said.

Eve loved her new dress. It was prom-worthy, if she did say so herself – short, with a boned bodice and a little tulle showing below the hem.

'Do you think I'm too dressed up?' Eve asked. 'I know Luke told me to, but guys and girls don't really have the same idea about what dressed up is. Maybe he just meant I shouldn't wear jeans.'

'If you are, Luke will just have to take whatever he has planned up a notch,' Jess replied. 'Oh, I heard some gossip today.'

'And you waited until now to tell me?' Eve demanded, mock angry.

'We've been busy primping,' Jess reminded her. She moved over to her dresser and dabbed on some FlowerBomb perfume.

'Well, tell me now, you tease,' Eve said.

'I heard that Simon has a date. He's going to the prom!' Jess exclaimed.

'That's hard to picture,' Eve said. 'But good for him. Who's the girl?'

'Someone he met in that Russian class he's taking,' Jess answered.

'Do you think they'll bring big, musty books?' Eve asked.

'If they do, that just means they're perfect for each other. I feel so bad about blaming Simon for all that stuff. I've already told Seth that I'm asking Simon for a dance.'

Eve grinned. 'Good for you! Take a picture with him too. I want to see.'

Jess gave a twirl. 'Eve! I'm going to the prom!' she exclaimed, as if she'd just realized it.

And Eve didn't feel even a mini-panglet. 'Jess! I'm going out with Luke!' She gave a twirl of her own. Who would have thought a few days ago that she'd ever feel like twirling again? About anything!

'We're still going to do our prom double-date thing,' Jess said. 'Only three years until our own Senior Prom.'

Eve smiled. 'I know! And think of the shopping we'll be forced to do.'

'Think of the—'

A knock on the door interrupted Jess. 'Come in,' Jess called.

Peter entered, holding a camera. 'Mom wants pictures of you both up here. She sent me because she says she can't figure out all the buttons.' He shook his head.

Eve noticed Peter had flecks of white paint on his shirt, jeans, and even in his hair. 'What have you been up to, messy?' she teased, so glad Peter was here for her *to* tease. He seemed to have forgotten pretty much everything that he'd done while possessed, but Jess said sometimes he'd stare off into space with a sickened expression on his face.

'I was painting the playhouse in the backyard,' he answered.

'The playhouse? Why? You thinking of having a party?' Jess joked.

He shook his head, and his eyes got kind of unfocused. Eve thought she was seeing the expression Jess had told her about. 'I just . . . I went out there – I'm not even sure why – and there was blood spattered on the walls and floors.' He hesitated, swallowing hard a few times. 'I'm thinking maybe a cat killed a bird in there or something. Even though I didn't find a bird.'

'The cat probably took it. They like to leave birds on the porch as presents for their owners,' Eve said quickly. She glanced at Jess and they had a telefriendic moment. Eve was sure Jess was thinking exactly what she was – that the playhouse had to be where Peter killed Pumpkin and maybe all the other animals.

'It's great you got it fixed up, Peter,' Jess said, with too much enthusiasm. 'Maybe the little cousins will visit this summer and use it.' She looped her arm around Eve's shoulders. 'Now, picture please.'

Eve and Jess gave Peter a bunch of poses. 'I have more than enough for a magazine,' he finally said. 'I'll go show Mom.'

'I'll definitely need some of those pics for my hatbox,' Jess said. 'Evie, I can't believe Alanna almost destroyed our friendship.'

'*Almost* is the key word,' Eve answered. 'You came after me when I ran to the city, even when Alanna had done everything she could to make you hate me.'

Jess nodded, looking as thought she might cry. Eve pointed at her. 'Don't you dare. Waterproof mascara is never really completely waterproof.'

'I won't,' Jess promised. 'If I start to get teary, we can just talk some more about Alanna. That will make us way too mad to cry.'

'I actually do have a little Alanna news,' Eve said. 'Luke talked to Callum this morning. The Order has figured out that Alanna was a night-hag. That's a kind of demon who smothers people in their sleep. But I guess she got ambitious. You heard her during our smack-down. It's like she wanted to start a demon union.'

'That's something I don't even want to try to imagine.' Jess made a small adjustment to chain of the pink heart pendant. 'What do you think she's been doing in the hundred years since your great-great-great trapped her in that body? Which was way too good a body to trap a demon in, if you ask me.'

'I guess the Order just had info for the past twenty years or so. She had ID as Alanna, birth certificate, college transcripts, all that,' Eve answered. 'She probably kept moving around, changing identities, waiting for me to go Witch so she could kill me. She couldn't access her demon powers, so she couldn't get into too much trouble.'

The doorbell rang, and Eve and Jess exchanged gleeful smiles. 'That's gotta be our guys,' Eve exclaimed. Luke was picking her up at Jess's because they'd wanted to get ready together, even though they were going out separately.

'Well, let's go show them our gorgeous selves,' Jess replied.

They answered the door together, Eve's arm wrapped around Jess's waist. Luke and Seth stood on the porch. The expression on Luke's face sent tingles – almost like her power – running through Eve. He looked dazzled. That was the only word for it. Dazzled.

And she definitely wasn't too dressed up. Luke was in a suit and tie. He was pretty dazzling himself.

'You both look awesome,' Luke said, his eyes on Eve.

'Don't try and pretend you even looked at me,' Jess teased.

'I don't want him looking at you anyway,' Seth said with a grin. Eve finally managed a glance at him. The tux Jess had chosen was exactly right – three button had definitely been the way to go. 'I'm the only one who should get to see you in that dress.'

'Remember what I told you about Simon,' Jess said. 'He gets a dance. If he wants one.'

'Everyone's going to want one,' Seth told her.

'He's pretty cute when he's jealous,' Eve teased.

'Isn't he?' answered Jess.

'Just adorable,' Luke joked.

Together, the two couples strolled down the drive. A limo was waiting for Seth and Jess. Eve didn't feel anything remotely pang-ish as they climbed inside, Mr and Mrs Meredith taking photos.

'Have a fantastic time,' Eve called as the driver prepared to shut the door. 'And an amazing one. And a wonderful one. And a—'

Jess held up one hand, stopping her list. 'I'll have the best time I possibly can without my best friend there,' she promised. The driver closed the door and got back behind the wheel. Eve and Jess watched until the limo disappeared round the corner.

'So are we ready to go?' Luke asked.

'Go where?' Eve said.

'Do I need to get you a dictionary?' Luke shook his head. 'I thought you knew the word "surprise", but clearly not.'

'Fine. Wherever we're going, I'm ready,' Eve told him. And she was. Eve was the Deepdene Witch, and there was nothing she couldn't handle – with a little help from her friends.

Not that she was expecting to have to go all Witch that night. She was expecting to go all girlfriend.